Contents

Join the crew!

Andromeda Spaceways is looking for energetic and motivated people to be part of the ASM editorial team.

Perhaps you'd like to be a reader and assess story submissions, maybe you'd like to create book reviews, do some copy-editing, proofing, show off your marketing skills or maybe you'd just like to learn more about how to publish a magazine.

There's lots to do including editing, layout, artwork, eBook production, distribution and general administration. How much you want to do is up to you. We'd love to hear from you.

For more information, go to
https://andromedaspaceways.com/recruitment/

Andromeda Spaceways Magazine

SCIENCE FICTION, FANTASY AND HORROR

Best Stories: Vol. 4

PUBLISHED BY

ANDROMEDA SPACEWAYS PUBLISHING INCORPORATED

WWW.ANDROMEDASPACEWAYS.COM

FEBRUARY 2021

Andromeda Spaceways Magazine
ISBN 78-0-6481117-3-3
RRP AUD$19.95*
Published by Andromeda Spaceways Publishing Incorporated.

All general communications should be sent to: asimeditor@gmail.com.

*Available in Print-only format and can be purchased from the website.
www.andromedaspaceways.com

Printed by IngramSpark, www.ingramspark.com

Design and Layout: Wayne Harris and Joel Schanke

Subscriptions to Andromeda Spaceways Magazine
Buy a First Class Subscription ticket and get brand-new fiction—in EPUB, MOBI or PDF formats. We'll also throw in some members-only goodies for you to enjoy. Make your way to https://www.andromedaspaceways.com/subscribe/ to get your subscription.

If you have any queries about a current subscription, please email accounts@ andromedaspaceways.com.

Submissions
ASM is open to science fiction, fantasy and supernatural horror works up to 10,000 words in length. All submissions must be via the website at https://andromedaspaceways.com/submissions-manager/. Please read the full submissions guidelines at https://andromedaspaceways.com/submissions-manager/ before submitting.

Advertising rates and specifications are available at:
www.andromedaspaceways.com/contact-us/advertising/

The Caregiver

Featured in Issue #77

...Jim Gourley

Father dies first. Mother is too weak to bury him. The drugs don't suppress the allergen anymore. Her lungs are calcifying. Every day her breath gets a little shorter. If she takes the gulp of air her body screams for, her chest cavity will crack like burnt paper. She would welcome the release from the slow panic of asphyxia. But she has to hold on for the baby's sake. So that's what she does.

They were the first couple to get pregnant. The others were months behind and the allergen finished the women before they came to full term. Mother and father assumed the baby wouldn't last. They braced for the cruelty of just barely outliving their child. But two months went by, then three. Then they faced a worse cruelty. This atmosphere is not alien to the child. Instead of suffocating, she will starve.

Unless, father had said. *There's a chance.* The colony's artificial intelligence. All but the most essential med lab equipment. Everything was committed to the effort. Father validated motor functions and logic pathways the day before he died. Only mother remains to teach a robot how to be a parent. She hasn't nearly enough time. How do you upload instinct? What is the command prompt for motherhood?

Just love her. Her voice is barely more than sand racing across the outer habitat wall in the windy season.

The robot cannot feel love. Please specify directives.

Mother closes her eyes. Her lungs will break open if she sobs. *Emulate human behaviours and acts associated with love.*

Define parameters.

Keep her safe from physical harm. Don't let her out of your sight unless it's essential. Promote her emotional well-being. Don't lie to her.

There is so much more to say, but she is exhausted. She needs rest before she can continue.

She dies in her sleep, the baby in her arms. Cambria would have been the fourth colony beyond Earth. It collapses in just 27 months. People across the universe watch the tragedy unfold from the isolation of their worlds. Adrift on their little lifeboat orbs, all they can send now are thoughts and prayers. Anything of substance is constrained by physics and economics. Tian has yet to reach industrial maturity. Columbia is closer by a few lightyears. Earth has the most robust fleet. No matter how or where from, it will be twelve years before the child feels another human's touch.

The baby cries. Her caregiver cradles her for the first time. A synthetic surrogate, it is the new Pieta for the interstellar age. The baby falls back asleep. The robot buries the mother and child-proofs the habitat.

The baby frequently cries through the night, though it wants for nothing. For six months the robot keeps uninterrupted vigil. Its arms hold her small body without feeling bone-deep weariness. It sterilises bottles and washes diapers without desperate bouts of insecurity or loneliness. It listens to hours of wailing without the unspeakable secret regret that creeps into every mother's mind. It cradles and feeds and hums lullabies without any sense of joy or affection.

The baby rejects another bottle. The formula is precious and must be preserved. The robot returns it to the warmer. The bottle will not fit. The robot twists it one way and another. The baby cries more frantically. The robot focuses on the task even as the child begins to writhe in its arm. Finally, the bottle seats in the warmer. The robot wipes a tear. The baby grabs the finger and sucks on it. The robot turns on a hot plate, changes arms, puts its other hand on the hot surface. The baby no longer cries. For the next six months, the robot continues to hold the baby this way, alternating arms and warming its hands to feel more human-like. The baby stops crying. The scent of heated alloys becomes soothing to her. She eats and sleeps better.

The baby has its first birthday.

The robot maintains the vigil through teething, earaches, and colds. It downloads and implements all the best practices to teach motor functions and early cognition. The child exceeds all developmental standards at the eighteen-month milestone. The robot receives a message from Earth. A rescue ship has departed. Because the planetary environment is lethal to humans, special precautions will be emplaced during retrieval. The robot is given new directives and parameters. Priority one: Care for the child. Priority two: research and, if possible, resolve the allergen pathology. All data relevant to priorities one and two must be secured. The robot cannot feel suspicious or perceive ulterior motives.

Baba. The girl says her first word. It is the name she gives the robot. The robot deduces it comes from the child's favourite book, about an elephant. A month later the child says her own name for the first time. *Amari.*

Amari turns two. Baba bakes a small cake. The robot reserved enough chocolate from the colony's supplies to ice and decorate ten cakes like this one. It has thought of almost everything in advance.

Amari learns new words. *No. I don't want to. Baba do it. I don't want peas! I want cookies!* Baba meets each protest with uncompromising politeness, counters each tantrum with merciless serenity.

Take your vitamin, Amari.

No! I want a cookie!

The vitamin is important to bone growth and liver function. Please eat it.

I want a cookie!

If I give you a cookie, will you eat the vitamin?

Yes!

Baba gives Amari a cookie. Amari does not eat the vitamin. Baba comprehends that Amari has lied.

Amari, did you make this mess?

No.

Amari, are you climbing out of your bed?

No.

Amari, do you need a new diaper?

No.

It takes Baba six months to develop subroutines and compile enough data to discern a lie from the truth. It takes another three months to make Amari understand that lying is bad, and another three to convince her she will be caught and punished. Robot and child learn together through a process of error and trial.

Amari turns three. She can read on her own. Her new favorite book is *The Little Prince*. She watches Baba tend the fields and asks if there are bad trees that will break their planet.

No, Amari. Our planet is too big for the plants to hurt it.

But there are bad plants.

The plants are not bad. The plants make dust that causes people to get sick. We just need to figure out how to make the people better.

Amari frowns. *How?*

I must study the pollen.

I want to help!

You help by not getting sick, Amari. In time I will understand why everyone else got sick and you didn't.

And then we can get my mommy back?

No, Amari. We cannot get her back.

Baba play with me.

The game is hide-and-seek. Baba hides where it can keep sight of Amari. It cannot break its directive to protect the child. *Ha! You're a bad hider! Find me now! Count!*

Baba counts. It cannot block its optical sensors. It walks to where Amari is hiding behind a rock. *No!*

Don't look at me! Count again!

Baba starts to count again. *No! Stop looking!*

Baba cannot stop. Baba has to watch. Mommy said Baba must always watch.

Mommy said? When?

Three years ago.

Where is she now?

Mommy is dead.

Amari cries. The game is over.

Baba realizes a conflict in directives. Tell the truth. Protect the child's emotional well-being. Baba must learn to tell the truth less, or say it more gently. In the meantime, cookies make Amari feel better and board games offer a safe way to play. Baba determines that adjusting difficulty levels is an acceptable means of adapting within the constraints of honesty.

Amari turns four. She can almost beat Baba at Memory. Baba can almost tie Amari at I-Doubt-It. They split games of Uno.

Amari exits her room one day with her mother's dress wrapped around her. *Baba! Today the people come! Get dressed!*

Baba does not understand. No, Amari. No one is coming for many years.

No, no! Pretend!

Baba can simulate the permutations of more than eight quintillion simultaneous genetic combinations in a second. It cannot pretend. It follows the child and does her bidding. Amari drapes clothes over the robot and throws all the tools out of a trunk.

This is the spaceship. Get in, Baba! Let's go to Earth!

I cannot fit in the rescue ship.

Amari looks over her shoulder at the box, then to Baba. *I can't go without you! Let's make the ship bigger.*

Baba pauses for a second to consider the permutations of Amari's statement and its directives. Its processor hums from the effort. Amari hears the sound and notices the lights within its chest glow a little brighter for a moment. She interprets this as love.

The robot takes a compass from the scattered equipment. You do not need to take all of me. This is my memory. It is all the things I know about you. So long as you have my memory, I will always go with you. Keep it safe.

Amari hangs the compass around her neck and smiles. She faces forward and makes rocket engine noises. In her mind, she is blasting away from this lonely place of dying. She pretends gravity pulls her back into the seat, trying to hold her back. Baba assesses that it has successfully told a gentle truth.

Amari gets to Earth. She does not know what to pretend about life there. Baba offers to explain, but Amari is done pretending now. *I love you, Baba.*

Baba does not feel or understand love. Baba must be honest. Baba must protect the child's emotional well-being. It pauses again.

Would you like a cookie?

Amari turns five. Baba bakes another cake and gives her a soccer ball and her very own tablet computer. Amari's face darkens when she unwraps the presents. Something has occurred to her.

Is that the cake I had last year?

It is a new cake, identical in design to the last one.

This ball and this computer were already here. They belonged to someone else.

Our stockpiles are limited to whatever arrived with the initial logistics support module. No one owned these items. They were spares.

I don't want them.

Would you like something else?

No. All of these things are from dead people and I don't want them.

These items came directly from the stockpile. They have never been used—

I don't want them!

Amari goes to her room. She doesn't want to talk. She doesn't want to read books or do chores. She responds to Baba's admonitions with impolite facial expressions. Her speech becomes limited to commentary on how stupid various things are. The plants they raise for her nourishment are stupid. The shelter that keeps them safe during the windy season is stupid. Books and arithmetic are stupid. Board games are stupid.

Amari, did you take a cookie from the jar?

No.

That is a lie, Amari. I can tell. I know you took a cookie.

Then why did you ask?

It is important for you to learn honesty and to apologize for breaking rules.

Amari makes an impolite face.

If you cannot admit your guilt and apologize, I will stop making cookies.

Go ahead. I don't want your stupid cookies.

Amari grows restless. Her sixth birthday is even worse than her fifth.

Those markers where Mommy and Daddy are buried are stupid. No one is ever going to come see them.

That is not necessarily true. The allergen—

This whole planet is stupid. They were stupid for coming here.

Amari, you mustn't say such things.

You're the stupidest!

Baba turns to correct the child. Amari runs away. She is faster and more agile than Baba. She clambers a rocky hillside and taunts the robot. Baba assesses the terrain is too steep to negotiate. The robot stands at the base of the hill for twenty minutes while Amari pounds her fist against the world below her and screams at the heavens above.

When she is done, Amari sees Baba through her tears. The robot is waiting at the bottom of the hill without judgment, or complaint, or anger. She doesn't see a fissure in one of the rocks. Amari catches her foot and spills eight feet. Her body comes to rest in a grotesque position. Baba assesses the danger of attempting to climb up to Amari as severe. Amari whimpers. She does not answer when called.

Baba labors up the hill. Amari's arm is broken in two places and she is unconscious. Baba cradles the girl in one arm and attempts to slide back down. It slips and falls back. The dirt scratches its coating. A rock dents the torso casing. Baba's free arm becomes lodged in another fissure. There is nowhere to put Amari down so it can free its arm. It must hold on for the well-being of the child. So that's what it does.

Baba wrenches back and twists. The elbow joint pops and they are free again. The child nuzzles fitfully against her broken robot's chest. The robot meticulously guards the child's broken parts from further pain.

Amari wakes up to her arm in a cast and Baba watching over her. She does not cry until she sees Baba's arm.

I'm sorry. Please don't hate me.

I will never hate you.

I'm sorry.

I forgive you.

This is Baba's first outright lie. Baba cannot forgive Amari because Baba does not get angry or assign blame. But the child needs to receive forgiveness, so the robot offers it. Amari becomes sick whenever she looks at the grizzled bobtail of wires and metal hanging down from Baba's arm. She keeps asking Baba if it hurts.

Did you already lose all your blood? I don't want you to die.

I do not have blood. I cannot die.

You said everyone has blood. You said I was born with special blood when you took some out with the needle.

All humans have blood. Robots do not. Robots are not born. They are assembled. Your father and mother assembled me.

But if your mommy and daddy are my mommy and daddy, then they died... which means you can die!

Baba does not know how to make Amari understand. It takes Amari to a terminal and unlocks a video log of a man assembling a robot. His skin is blue and there are beet-colored circles under his eyes. He keeps working though he is in obvious discomfort.

Do you understand now? I was built. I am a robot. I cannot die or feel pain.

Was that daddy?

Yes.

Are there more videos of him? Are there videos of mommy?

Baba's processor hums in thought and its chest glow. Amari puts her hand over Baba's chest.

I miss them, too.

Baba reviews terabytes of peer-reviewed literature on early childhood development and trauma in a few moments.

Yes, there are more videos.

Can I see them?

Not now.

Why?

They were very sick. The videos would upset you. Your parents would not want that right now.

Baba, will you ever get sick?

No.

You're never going to leave me?

No.

Amari has Baba sign her cast. The robot does not know what to write, so it asks Amari. The robot's chest glows and hums in response to the girl's request. Baba writes across the length of the cast in beautiful, exacting cursive. Amari surrounds the message with flowers and hearts. When it comes off, she places it in a box under her bed as a keepsake.

Could you reattach your arm if I got it back?

Please make no attempt to retrieve the arm. It is too dangerous.

But you only have one arm and it's my fault.

You are forgiven.

But it's not right you have to be this way.

I can perform all motor-function tasks equally well with either hand. The damage has negligible impact on my productivity.

I would be careful.

Amari, if you tried to retrieve my arm against my wishes, I would be hurt and disappointed. I would not forgive you. If you were to get hurt again I could not help you. I would be alone without you.

More lies. In the interest of the child's well-being.

I won't go. I promise. I love you, Baba.

Rest. When you wake up we will make cookies.

The child rests and helps to make cookies. She opens the oven door while the robot puts the pan in. The smell of dough and heated alloy makes her smile. She learns how to tend the fields. She helps to take pollen samples. She inspects her blood for antigens. She helps to clean. She learns to do all of these things with the same efficient motions as the robot. With the same speech patterns and vocabulary. With the same patience. Like robot, like daughter.

Amari grows more mature, more methodical, more mechanical. Baba puts another cake on the table.

Baba, I am nine years old.

Yes. Happy birthday.

I have been here nine years.

Would you like to blow out the candles?

Baba, I would like to see the videos of my parents.

You are not yet old enough. They were very sick. They were suffering. It would be an unpleasant experience for you.

I have been conditioned to unpleasant experiences for nine years, Baba. I am well-adjusted to them.

Baba has never heard this before. Based on the structure and thought of the child's argument, Baba assesses that she is old enough.

They watch the videos. Mom holds the baby and utters words Amari has never heard.

I love you, Amari.

Amari closes her eyes and exhales. She breathes out something heavy and unpleasant that has weighed her down for nearly her entire life.

I love you. Mom's voice is warm and melodic. *I love you.* Amari wants to dance to it.

They keep watching. Baba materializes on a work table. Father deteriorates. Mom demonstrates how to feed the baby as Baba stands next to her. She explains how to change a diaper from a wheelchair, how to swaddle and bathe from her bed. Amari watches the circles under her mom's eyes run deeper into the sockets, the corners of her mouth pull tighter in discomfort. She keeps trying.

I love you. It sounds like sand blowing across the habitat walls in the windy season, but Amari can still make out the words.

Amari watches Baba take her from Mom's arms for the last time. Even in that moment, she knows Mom is still trying. Amari holds tight to Baba.

The windy season comes early this year. Amari hears Mom's ghost wandering the valley. There's a rhythm in the beating of the wind against the walls, a melody in the creaking of the structure's joints. Mom is trying to say *I love you.* Amari asks if she can sleep with Baba. The robot will not be able to perform several evening maintenance items. Baba does not sleep. The robot lies down and puts an arm over Amari. The atmosphere roils around them. Their foster world whirls on its axis and twists around its sun like a leaf caught in a storm drain.

The wind storm lasts four days. They stay huddled in the shelter. Baba plans maintenance checks each night, but Amari asks the robot to keep her company. Amari wakes one night and sits up. Something is wrong. Mother's voice sounds different. She tries to tell Baba, but the robot insists it is just a dream. Baba cannot make believe, so Amari cannot make it understand. The building was meant to be a temporary shelter and it has stood for ten years. Baba has not done maintenance checks for four nights.

Mother's ghost groans. The roof joist snaps. An aluminum bar tears and the wall next to them shears away as if in the teeth of a wild animal. They are swarmed by angry debris. Baba throws itself on top of Amari.

The storm passes. Amari crawls out from under Baba to find the habitat completely destroyed. The composite skin dangles in shreds from skewers of broken frame. It looks like the carcass of some picked-over leviathan. Baba is tangled in the spars of its rib cage. Amari fights through her fear to gather tools. It takes several hours for her to cut away enough of the metal to free Baba. Over and over, they have the same conversation.

I'm sorry.

It is not your fault.

If I hadn't asked you to stay with me…

This could not have been prevented. Maintenance checks would not have led me to discover the

structure failing.

Another lie. It is necessary to protect her from trauma.

Please be alright.

Everything will be fine.

Baba is uncertain if that is true. It has already performed a self-diagnostic. There is an anomaly.

They go to the lab. Baba instructs Amari to examine it for damage. Take out these screws. How do the wires look? Good. Now remove the thoracic plate. Use the pliers if you must. See the four tubes running to my core processor housing? Do you see any liquid?

Yes. The blue tube is dripping fast.

That explains the anomaly. One of the primary capillaries feeding Baba's redox-based liquid quantum computer lost pressure. Baba is leaking brain fluid.

Amari receives very important instructions. Get a new tube. Cut it to similar length. I will power off and you can restart me once you have replaced the tubes. Do it quickly. Save as much fluid as you can.

The whole procedure takes less than two minutes. Amari catches several milliliters of the precious fluid in a vial. Baba returns it to the appropriate reservoir. Capacity is now at thirty-seven percent. Baba calculates the degradation rate at current performance levels. Eighteen months. It recalculates with power saving strategies. Two years. It calculates again with regular shutdowns. Again after closing subroutines. Again with higher thresholds for memory access during decision-making processes. Thirty-two months. Rescuers will not arrive for forty-eight months. Baba must find a way, so it keeps trying.

Are you okay, Baba? Did it work?

Baba simulates the permutations of the necessary measures and their consequences in less than a second. It will take Amari longer. Baba recalculates again, this time factoring for the girl. Then it tells another lie.

Yes. You did wonderfully. I must take steps to fully recover. I will power off at night now. It will help if you manually power me on in the morning.

I can do that.

Baba never says how long it will take to fully recover. Amari never asks. After a few weeks, the process becomes routine. Off. On. Off. On.

The windy season gives way to harvest season. Amari frowns at Baba one morning. *That's a sickle, Baba. We need the hoe, don't we?*

Winds give way to planting season, not harvest. It is a small error. Baba exchanges for the hoe.

The next week Baba seizes while powering on. It reboots. Baba says once in eleven years is within system tolerances. The same thing happens again three days later.

Baba, what is happening to you?

Everything is fine.

Baba, it distresses me to know you are lying.

Amari listens to lengthy technical explanations. The robot speaks in choppy sentences fraught with rates and percentages.

You're dying.

I cannot die.

Amari wipes her face with both hands. She resents having to use the technical language. *Your processor is approaching catastrophic failure.*

Yes. My system performance is declining. Power management strategies will prolong my service life to the safe date.

Amari has never heard these words before. *Define the term 'safe date'.*

Fourteen days prior to rescue ship arrival.

Amari's lower lip trembles. *What…* she has to begin again. *What will your status be when the rescue ship arrives?*

The processor core will experience acute degradation. The system will be compromised.

Amari nods. *Thank you. I understand. We will work on strategies tomorrow.*

The principal directives are to care for you and study the allergen. All other considerations are ancillary.

I would like you to begin your power-down cycle now, Baba.

Understood. Goodnight, Amari.

When the soft glow within Baba's carapace is gone, Amari throws her arms around it and lets go of her tears. *I love you, Baba.*

They do not talk about preparing for the ship's arrival. Amari is not ready to know how much time they have until the safe date.

Amari decides that Baba should have a birthday. She makes a cake with ten candles. The AI is much older than that, but Amari counts from the day the robot was activated. Amari makes the cake. The robot snuffs each candle out between its fingers. Amari detects the scent of singed alloy and feels warm inside.

This is supposed to be your cake. Your birthday is in two days.

My birthday wish is for us to celebrate yours.

Amari's birthday was two months ago. Something about Baba's processor degradation and the lengthened shutdowns are causing it to lose time. Amari considers the ramifications.

Baba, I would like to implement a new power saving strategy. From now on, I do not want you to come out to the field with me.

I should be with you if you have an accident with the machinery.

Monitor me using the cameras based on the observation tower. It will save some effort.

I concur.

Good. Assign yourself a new protocol not to leave the shelter unless I am in distress.

Amari has never told Baba to do anything before. Now with a single command she has made it homebound. Baba complies without judgment, or complaint, or anger. Amari always feels worse because of it.

Amari works the fields alone. She spends long hours in the sunlight until her skin glows. With each seed bag hauled and field implement heaved she grows lean and strong and radiant.

Inside the shelter, Baba's processor slowly diminishes. The light of the robot's mind dims. Amari has to make more rules. *Verify with me that it's time to cook before you try to make dinner. Do not engage the irrigation system controller. Do not use the ladder. Do not attempt repairs on electrical fixtures.*

Baba performed thousands of tasks every day to care for Amari. There are at least a thousand rules now, and for each one of them Amari has a new responsibility. She does not complain. She refuses to feel bone-deep weariness, or insecurity, or loneliness, or the resentment of coupling the energy of her youth to the care of one in decline. She has learned all this from Baba's example.

Amari observes the approach of her twelfth birthday. She does not want to make a cake, but she does it for the sake of helping the robot keep time. Baba has trouble pinching the candles. Its hand quivers too much to catch the flame just so. Amari holds the wrist steady as the robot extinguishes the flame.

She leans over the candles and takes a deep breath.

They must have a difficult conversation while Baba can still provide information. If Baba is to survive until the rescue day, it will have to be shut down indefinitely. Amari will need to know how to get them off the planet alone.

Baba, please explain the procedure for the rescue.

The ship will be here in approximately three-hundred days. It will transmit location data for a landing site. A lander with a small launch vehicle will land at that site. You will enter, follow instructions by radio, and wait until the launch window for the rescue ship's orbit. The craft will dock with the rescue ship. There will be room for an additional six-point-eight kilograms of personal effects.

Amari feels the words bite her chest.

What about you?

Do you remember the time we simulated your departure? I told you the rocket was not big enough for me.

We could have shut you down. You would have been okay.

The rescue was planned as quickly as possible. They didn't anticipate a planet they couldn't land on. The retrieval vehicle was retrofitted. Accommodating my full assembly was not a principal concern.

They never planned to get you. For the first time in years, Amari's voice sounds angry. *They never cared about you.*

They will save what is most important. Do you remember the compass?

Amari's face streams with tears. *Your memory drive.*

Yes. I have recorded everything. My entire experience on Cambria will survive.

I can load your memory to a new AI. A new robot.

No. The retrieval team will take the memory core. My data is of extreme scientific value. It will be used to discern what happened to the colony effort.

Discern what happened… The words taste alkaline.

Would it be possible to resume this discussion in two hours? Managing this conversation used more processing power than normal.

Amari swallows hard. Baba feels itself slipping.

Yes, of course. Rest.

The lights in Baba's torso dim. Amari waits until they grow dark and cold, then goes outside. She kicks a rock formation and screams into space.

Amari sits with Baba at the end of each day. Their conversations become more labored.

I think I've isolated the calcification mechanism. It's not chemical. There's an odd protein in the pollen itself. It interferes with cilia growth at the mitochondrial level—

I have compiled a list of common social behaviors perceived as inappropriate or rude in public spaces. It is imperative to understand these when you arrive on Earth.

You told me about those yesterday, Baba. We do not have to do it again. I saw some haze out east today. Might mean an early windy season. I think I'll dust the solar panels tomorrow, just to make sure we get a good charge on the batteries.

There may be men on the rescue craft. You have never interacted with one before. Interactions between human males and females are more complex than I comprehend. However, certain general principles will be valuable to you for—

If there is an early windy season the rescue ship may have to wait an extended period for a recovery window.

Then perhaps we should review retrieval procedures. The lander will—

Amari pounds her fists against her forehead.

I don't want to talk about the stupid lander or its stupid procedures! I don't want to go! I want to stay here with you!

You cannot stay here, Amari. Even if you did, I will cease to function.

You said you would never leave me.

I will not leave you. You will leave me.

Amari's face contorts. Baba cannot assess whether the girl is making an impolite face, so it cannot formulate a response. The girl falls asleep. The robot powers itself down shortly after. Days pass. Amari simply directs Baba to cease discussions of Earth or retrieval. She cannot bear the thought of moving on without knowing how to let go.

The windy season does not come early. The rescue ship does. The computer sends a communication alert. Amari plays the message. There is no video. Amari hears a woman's voice.

"Hi, Amari. How are you? My name's Doctor Karen. I'm a doctor and I'm here to help. Me and my friends have come in a spaceship from Earth to help. We're all excited to see you and we want to know if you're doing alright. Can you please send us a message back?"

Amari has to play the message several times to understand it. The woman speaks with an accent. She uses contractions and odd sentence structure. She talks so *fast.*

Amari sends her response: *Your arrival was not anticipated for another three weeks. I request a one hundred-twenty- hour delay before initiating retrieval operations.*

The ship responds thirty minutes later.

"I know this is a difficult time for you, Amari. Is there anything you want to talk about?"

There are no difficulties. I had not planned to prepare for departure for another three days. I request time to adequately prepare.

"We brought plenty of things with us just for you, Amari. If there is a special toy or game you have trouble leaving, let me know and if we don't have one here I'll see if we can make one."

Amari almost thinks that the woman on the radio is stupid for thinking she would have an emotional attachment to a toy. Then she realizes the woman is using her degrees and certifications to talk about Baba indirectly. Amari realizes the woman is dishonest… and stupid. She can't be the one in charge. Amari can use that.

I am conducting a test on the allergen. If my hypothesis proves correct, then it may have value to producing a cure. I request time to complete the test.

The test is a lie, but the hypothesis is not. Amari has learned from Baba that this is the most effective way to lie. There is a long delay on the radio while the child expert finds someone with more appropriate certifications.

"That could be dangerous, Amari. If we wait, there could be wind storms that make us wait even longer, and then we have a problem making sure there's enough food for the trip back. We don't want to risk your safety, do we?"

Understood. Barometric readings give no indication of high winds occurring in the next eight days. I request a ninety-six-hour delay to allow for pre-departure preparation.

"Are you asking for the delay so you can say goodbye to Baba?"

The sound of the woman's voice saying Baba's name makes Amari angry.

Negative. I have not yet prepared my personal effects.

There is a long silence. The rescue ship keys the microphone twice without saying anything before the woman comes back.

"Amari, would seventy-two hours be enough to complete the test, prepare the memory drive and assemble personal effects? We can give you ninety-six if you really need, but the captain is very concerned about your safety. We all are."

Thank you for your concern. Ninety-six hours will be sufficient. Please advise when the lander is in position.

Amari signs off. She has clawed back four days. The end that never should have come is still coming sooner than it should.

Baba, may I ask you a question?

Of course.

I have an ethical dilemma. You have said that I must take your memory drive to the rescue crew. The drive would give researchers full access to all information about the allergen. It would also give full access to all recordings of private moments, actions, and thoughts throughout my entire life. It would represent an extraordinary invasion of my privacy.

The dilemma is a conflict between two primary directives: serve the scientific mission and preserve your emotional and physical well-being.

Yes. Amari smiles and wipes a tear away. Baba has always been so clear about things. So direct. The conversation with the space woman has made Amari realize just how much she will miss the way Baba understands her. *If you had to decide between my well-being and the scientific directive, what would you choose?*

I no longer have the capacity for such high-level ethical judgments. My system is too degraded to effectively assess ill-defined parameters. I would defer to your assessment.

Defer to me?

You have demonstrated a high level of psychological maturity, and it is a logical choice because the decision impacts you so directly.

One of my… directives is to do what you… evaluate as the best course of action.

I cannot make an assessment.

Please, Baba. I need your help. This is… an unpleasant experience for me.

You are well-adjusted to unpleasant experiences. I am confident that you will negotiate the assessment process in a manner and with results that satisfy your conditions. I apologize. I must power down.

It takes Amari forty-eight hours to make her decision. Another sixteen to determine it satisfies her conditions. She notifies the retrieval ship crew that she will be ready to launch on time. It is a lie. She will never be ready.

Hello, Baba.

Hello, Amari. I perceive that more than sixty hours have passed since I powered down. Is there a problem? I had planned to bake cookies for your departure. We can still do that if there is time.

That will not be necessary. There is no problem. I had to prepare to leave and there was the ethical dilemma to reconcile. I needed time to consider directives.

I understand. What did you decide?

I would rather not say. I don't want you to be angry with me.

I could never be angry with you.

Never?

Never.

May I just say then that I am very satisfied with my choice.

That is all that matters.

I am leaving tonight, Baba. We will not speak again.

Based on the data I retrieved on human children and my observations of your development over the last twelve years, I assess that you will succeed in any endeavors you may choose in your life.

Thank you, Baba.

Amari waits, hoping that Baba will say something—say *one* thing. But it cannot. It did, once. Once was enough.

You may power down at your discretion, Baba.

Be sure to follow all safety instructions during the launch sequence. Goodbye, Amari.

The girl watches the warm light inside the carapace fade. The gentle hum within lowers its tone and fades to silence.

I love you, Mom.

The robot dies. The girl buries it beside the father and carries out pre-flight checks.

Telemetry confirms that she has carried six-point-oh-seven kilograms on board. Amari hears the jealous ghosts of long-dead colonists roar underneath her. They press on the ship and rock it back and forth, demanding to be let in. A moment later the lonely world that was home drains out of the window beside her. Amari is pressed into her seat by grief. She is surrounded by hot light, then unnatural blue, then a darkness so black that it must be make-believe. The craft comes to a halt with a sickening thud. There comes a hollow knocking, a metallic creak. Amari hears voices and is gripped by fear.

The expert space woman appears. Another one follows her in. Amari is welcomed. She is told she is safe, though she does not feel it. The people are hard to understand. They speak in a way she is not used to. She asks them to slow down. Enunciate.

The memory drives? Do you have them?

No.

You were told to bring them. They were very important.

That is why I left them.

The space women look at each other in aggravated despair. Amari sees that they don't understand. It is not much of a lie to say she is too exhausted to explain herself.

The ship loiters around Cambria for a time. Amari undergoes medical examination. She recoils from the warmth of human hands. A course is plotted. They go from transfer orbit to superluminal velocity. The journey will take three weeks or twelve years. They are going home or leaving it behind. Everything depends on the frame of reference.

The expert lady and the other crew members offer Amari cookies and colorful clothes and toys and games. She asks only for hot chocolate.

Amari goes to her room and comforts herself with the one item she brought from the surface. A robot's forearm rests peacefully in the embrace of a child's cast. She places the hot cup against the palm until she detects the scent of warm alloy. Amari turns the cast over and reads a message from long ago. She traces her finger lightly over the beautiful, exacting cursive, and remembers an ethical dilemma and a choice made. It is the one memory she carried with her. It is the memory of everything.

Love always, Baba.

The Orchard

Featured in Issue #76

...Ephiny Gale

I've been allocated the front seat because my twenty-eight-year-old legs fit better there. The rest of my competition, children between the ages of nine and fourteen, are comfortable in the back of the mini-van. They've spent the twenty-minute ride discussing school, Snapchat, Minecraft and a couple of other games or apps I haven't heard of and don't understand. I took a week off work for this, caught a train for almost three hours, spent a few hundred dollars in preparation. Now, I have a persistent stomach-ache and my considerable regret.

What on earth would appeal children of taking over a fruit orchard?

Finally, the van pulls up at a wrought iron gate; it seems enormous for a private property, almost twice my height. A thick crimson ribbon has been tied to each outer gate post and around the tight line of trees on each side of the gate. If it's supposed to welcome the kids, it's certainly a strange way of doing so; the ribbons are visibly faded and continue so far along the tree line that I can't see their other ends.

"This is where I leave you," announces Carina. She adjusts the ochre-coloured bandana tied underneath her braid. "Sorry I can't help you take the bags up."

"Wait," says Brandon, an older, freckled boy. "You're not coming with us?"

"Nope." Carina shuts the empty boot. "I'm not allowed past the gate. I've never seen any further than this." She winks at the kids, but I don't think she's joking. "You guys are lucky."

A couple of jaws drop. While we pick up our dusty luggage, Carina unlocks the gate with a large silver key. The four kids and I pass through, and it's secured again behind us.

The van reverses away.

We crest a hill and the farmhouse appears. I can't decide whether to be impressed or not—it's unusually wide for a house, with a smaller second storey and a large chimney sticking out of the centre of it all, like a blocky pyramid. The whole building looks bitsy, like the construction equivalent of a patchwork quilt, and all the parts seem well-made but needing some care. Smoke spirals cheerfully from the chimney.

"Whoa, check it out," says Brandon. The youngest kid, Jemima, is already running the last two hundred metres to the front door.

As the rest of us keep walking, a woman steps out onto the front porch, wearing a brown slip dress and crimson gloves. Jemima launches herself into the woman's arms and the woman catches her. I wonder if they know each other.

When the rest of us reach the porch, Jemima has settled back on the floor, and the woman reaches out to shake my hand. Her gloves are soft leather against my fingers. Her shoes are walking boots, and her simple dress laces up in the back like a loose corset. "I'm Bridgette," she says, "and this is my land. Welcome, all of you."

My other hand tightens around my suitcase handle. She's beautiful.

"Come in, come in," she says. "I'll show you to your rooms. Then we'll have some lunch."

Inside, Bridgette's décor is an eclectic mix of muted patterns, hanging plants, and expensive highlights. None of her sofas match. Flowering vines crawl over hardwood and shining geometric light fittings. I kind of love it here.

Past the living room and off a long corridor with botanical wallpaper, the kids and I have one small bedroom each. Mine is the last one. We're supposed to have twenty minutes to settle in between now and lunch, but I catch Bridgette with a touch to her shoulder.

"Listen," I say quietly, "there's obviously been some mistake. This was a competition for children, and it's ridiculous for me to even be here. I completely understand if you want me to go."

She's looking at me with a very tolerant smile—it makes me feel about as old as the kids. "There was no age limit on the competition, Emily. Mostly children were good at it, so mostly children got in." Her lips twitch towards a smirk. "Really, you should stay. You're the one at a disadvantage here. If you happen to win, you'll very much deserve it."

I am left to simmer in my embarrassment.

Lunch is essentially a friendly interview interspersed with food. I was expecting staff at the competition—administrators, cooks, gardeners—but we haven't seen anyone since Carina. Bridgette serves up a steaming vegetable soup with a slight chili kick. There are Christmas crackers on the table even though it's April; we pop them, and wear the paper crowns. We drink peach iced tea with plastic curly straws. Finally, we lock our five mobile phones in Bridgette's miniature safe, and it's time for a proper introduction to the competition.

Bridgette has the five of us line up beside the back door. One by one, she secures cotton blindfolds firmly over our eyes, so that I can't see anything beyond a sliver of my own feet. I hear the quiet *swish* of the back door sliding open, and then her gloved hand is secure in mine. I grasp Sierra's hand on the other side of me, and then we're pulled gently outside, all of us trailing over the grass after Bridgette like a human daisy chain.

"Now, when we arrive, you must all promise me not to move towards anything. Not to touch anything," Bridgette announces. "If you do, you will be immediately disqualified from the competition. Do you understand?"

Several variations of "yes" and "uh-huh" travel up from further down the line, and I quickly offer up my own. My brain is busy projecting half-a-dozen possibilities onto the backs of my eyelids about what exactly we might not be allowed to touch. I expect the children to start whispering again to one another, but now they're silent as snowfall.

Bridgette slows and then halts quicker than I am expecting, and I only barely prevent myself from running into her. The grounding warmth of her hand slips away. "Okay," she says after a moment. "You can take off your blindfolds."

At first, I think I'm looking at a painting. It takes my brain a few seconds to register the lack of canvas edges, the absence of brush strokes to understand that yes, all signs seem to point to this being real life.

The six of us stand in front of several rows of trees, unlike any I've seen or even imagined. Each one of them is large, at least four times my height and with trunks about six feet in diameter, but every one of them is a work of art. There's one tree with waxy honeycombs instead of bark, with a viscous waterfall of honey spiralling down from its canopy and down into the earth. Bees the size of my feet dart between levitating cherry blossom flowers, leaving behind trails of sparkling smoke in their wake. Another tree is made of gold and silver latticework, a rainbow of gems embedded throughout in a hundred different sizes. The smaller branches are hinged, and one opens to reveal a violet-coloured animal, somewhere between a red panda and a fox, with giant, six-sided gemstone eyes. It scuttles along, pries off a gem with its raptor-like claws and disappears with its prize into the hole it came from. Then there's a bone tree with a spiral of steps carved into the trunk. Strings of thousands of teeth drip down around it like a veil, like the leaves of a willow tree. Some of the teeth shine with chips or coatings of metal, like they had holes fixed with dental fillings.

And the trees keep stretching back and back, made of candy or muscle or patchwork cotton or surrounded with floating halos of water. My mind is reeling. One of the kids starts to swear and then pauses mid-word.

"I have filled about one third of this land already," says Bridgette, and I tear my eyes away to meet her gaze. "And I plan to fill another third. The last third will be filled by the winner of this competition, who will become my assistant and take care of this place in my absence, and who will inherit it after I die." She smiles at our gaping faces. I think I spot a twinkle in her caramel eyes. "Welcome to the orchard."

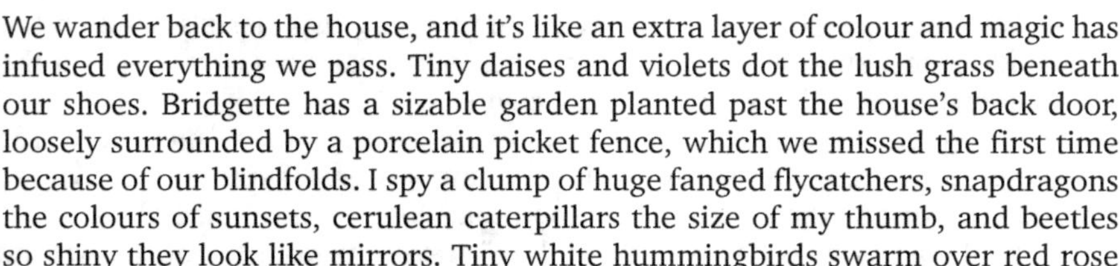

We wander back to the house, and it's like an extra layer of colour and magic has infused everything we pass. Tiny daises and violets dot the lush grass beneath our shoes. Bridgette has a sizable garden planted past the house's back door, loosely surrounded by a porcelain picket fence, which we missed the first time because of our blindfolds. I spy a clump of huge fanged flycatchers, snapdragons the colours of sunsets, cerulean caterpillars the size of my thumb, and beetles so shiny they look like mirrors. Tiny white hummingbirds swarm over red rose vines. Neon koi glow inside their semi-circular pond.

We pass through the sliding door again, and Bridgette puts the kettle on. She likes to answer questions with a warm cup in her hands, cross-legged on the most central couch.

Question: How do you win?

Answer: By being the last one left.

Question: How do you do that?

Answer: You make the best trees. You plant a small object in the ground, cover it with soil, and then run back so you don't get hurt by the tree growing. It happens very quickly.

Bridgette peels off her gloves to show us her visibly altered hands—shiny pale bolts of scar tissue cross her palms; she wasn't quick enough, the first couple of times—and then redresses them in leather.

Question: How do you know what makes the best trees?

Answer: You make an educated guess, based on what might come out. Don't just pick something because it looks cool; I want interesting, original, and personal choices. I asked you to bring a few important sentimental items with you for a reason. But please don't use anything you can't bear to part with, because you won't get it back.

Question: How long do we have?

Answer: The first round will be late tomorrow morning. Then we'll have lunch, and then Carina will arrive, and one of you will be leaving with her. So don't save your best seed until later—every time we plant anything, it really counts.

At this point there's a quiet bang, and a black, furry creature appears in Bridgette's living room via a medium-sized doggie door. As it gets closer, I can see it resembles an oversized cat, if cats had pouches on their bellies and six prehensile tails. It flicks its green eyes across the group of us, makes a squeaky sound like an inconvenienced fox, and uncurls one of its tails to drop a bird of paradise flower into Bridgette's lap.

Bridgette claps once with obvious delight, rocking back a little on the couch, and then runs her gloved fingers down its head and back. "Everyone, this is Marigold," she says. "She's very intelligent. I asked her, and a few others, to stay away until you'd seen the trees, but they should be coming back now." She scratches the side of Marigold's neck, eyes crinkling in affection. "Say hello, Marigold."

The cat eyes us again, and then arranges its tails in a very clear 'Hi' formation. The children gasp and squeal, and Jemima waves rapidly in response.

Bridgette lifts Marigold up on the couch with her. "You know most of the rules already, but there are a few more: you may be allowed to use something from this house or the gardens as a seed, but you must ask permission before taking it. And you're welcome to walk around the orchard, but don't go too near the trees, and if you're under eighteen then I expect you to do so in pairs."

She smiles slowly—a deeply satisfied smile—and then waves her hand to dismiss us. The children break into pairs and race back out towards the orchard. They're beaming and yelping and tapping each other like this is their first visit to Disneyland. They asked all the questions, and I asked none, paralysed on one of Bridgette's embroidered lounge chairs. Maybe this is part of what she meant by my disadvantage.

Bridgette's cup clinks down on the glass coffee table. I meet her eyes, expecting judgment, but they're gentle. "Emily," she says. "Goodness knows I don't get a lot of human visitors. But may I recommend a nap, then some more iced tea, and then a stroll around the orchard? After a big change, sometimes the brain just needs to re-set itself." She strokes a finger down between Marigold's eyes. "Turn it off and on again, so to speak. You'll have enough time."

The nap really does help. When I wake things feel clearer, more solid. I feel a little more like I'm meant to be here.

Bridgette is in the kitchen when I emerge, and there's talking and the watery clank of washing dishes, but the rest of the room looks empty and she's leaning on a counter away from the sink. Then she moves slightly, and I see flashes of movement and shine, like dragonfly wings. She motions me closer.

Tiny women the size of barbie dolls are scrubbing, dunking and drying our lunchtime dishes. Opalescent, insect-like wings protrude from their backs. "Fairies?" I whisper.

"That's not what they call themselves," says Bridgette. "But it's close enough. They are my very dear companions who look after the house and grounds. They also built the rooms you're staying in, and they are excellent conversationalists. Just don't expect them to be able to fly very far. They can get perhaps two feet off the ground. They're better at climbing."

A fairy dives under the dishwater for a moment to pull the plug, and then squeezes out her cobalt hair, while another wrings the dishcloth and springs up to hang the cloth over the tap, wings buzzing like a hummingbird. Bridgette pours me an iced tea, as promised.

The cobalt fairy holds out her doll-sized hand for me to take. "So pleased to meet you," she says, with a sharp accent I can't place and with a lower voice than I was expecting. "We're totally starved of new company."

I spend the next twenty minutes conversing with Bridgette and the fairies—or attempting to, because comprehension is sometimes a challenge for me when there are *mythical creatures* two feet away. I do learn that there's twelve of them in all, not just three, and that they've been here about four years, ever since Bridgette planted a lemongrass soap tree and part of what emerged was fairy-printed fabric. Now that fabric sits across Bridgette's kitchen window as butter-coloured curtains, and the fairies come and go as they please, merging into and out of their printed silhouettes.

Then I make a slow lap of the trees in the orchard, and my mind processes them better this time. The kids are still running around like it's a playground, but at least they're keeping a reasonable berth from the trees themselves. I examine each trunk, each canopy and root system as I pass, hoping for inspiration to strike. I wander between trees that look like living subway maps, trees with keys of every colour and shape knotted into their shoots, trees which just look like a column of pigeons stacked on top of one another, blinking and puffed up for the winter.

Back in my room, I lay out the contents of my suitcase across the cornflower blue carpet, and think, *what on earth is here that I can use?* I pass my eyes and hands over my more sentimental items a dozen times: a framed photo of my parents, a plastic cake knife (a prop from my favourite musical), a faded dog collar, a plastic ice-skating medal, and an old wedding ring. None of them seem like they would make half-decent trees.

Just as my brain threatens to shut down again, Timmy knocks nervously on my door and says, "Sierra's drawing trees on everyone in sharpie. Do you want one, too?"

I think of how bad that would be for my skin, plus the awful sharpie fumes. "Sure, I do."

We've rolled dice to determine the order we plant in: this time it's Timmy, Brandon, Jemima, me, and finally Sierra.

Bridgette's marked the exact spots where we're supposed to dig. Timmy finds the grass that's been coloured with Sierra's red sharpie. He crouches and opens his fist to reveal a sweaty USB stick, then buries it the way Bridgette has taught us: by digging a small hole in the dirt with both hands, placing his seed, and smoothing the soil back over the top.

As soon as the USB is covered, he bolts away. The ground has already started to vibrate under our feet, and there's an audible rumble for a moment before a great black tree erupts where Timmy was crouched seconds ago. It spirals out of the ground like a corkscrew, and as its growth slows, I can read the numbers that make up the trunk: a dense stream of ones and zeros. A very real crocodile runs up and down the spiral, jaw open to showcase its teeth. Back at home, Timmy had coded the first part of a smartphone game about a crocodile paddling through space.

"Don't worry," says Bridgette, sounding only mildly concerned. "It shouldn't leave the tree unless provoked."

We move on.

Brandon plants a cluster of interlocking colourful plastic, which I recognise as broken off from one of his nerf guns. The tree that sprouts is an intricate pillar of plastic, as if someone's designed a huge treehouse out of magical Lego. Its neon orange shutters wave gently in the wind.

Jemima plants a small metal container with a screw-top; perhaps it used to have lip gloss inside. I can't tell what she's filled it with now, but when the earth parts the tree that grows is made of water. Water in the shape of a fir tree, with fabric cartoon monsters floating inside. The monsters circle each other, gnashing their teeth and swiping their claws.

Then it's my turn, and I find my hands shaking as I plant my sorry excuse for a seed. I've wrapped the ribbon from my suitcase around the prop knife from my favourite musical, *Twelve Birthdays*. I stumble as I retreat. The tree that sprouts is a stunted mess of ribbon and melted pink plastic, barely as tall as I am, and I feel my entire body sink with embarrassment and disappointment.

But there's a small hole at the top of the tree, and slowly, so slowly, white fairy floss clouds begin to billow out. They puff and snowball until they've surrounded the tip of the tree like a dandelion head. And then music begins to seep from the hole, sweet and simple in the country air.

My fingernails gradually detract from where they've been digging into the heel of my palm.

Sierra is last. She's chosen her late father's cigarette lighter. The tree that emerges is made of patterned metal filigree, with flames burning inside like a giant metal lantern. Through the holes in the metal, we can see the fire flickering, changing colours to turn into fleeting images: an Indian man holding his daughters, sipping his coffee, adjusting his tie.

I glance at Sierra. "He gave up about ten years ago," she says, and I notice the tears on her cheeks. "But he carried it with him every day, anyway, in case it was needed. And then I did."

We watch for several minutes. We watch until Bridgette puts her hand on Sierra's shoulder, and we head inside for lunch.

Lunch, as prepared by the fairies, is roast lamb with mint jelly and cranberry sauce, and it's just about the best roast I've ever tasted. I expected the atmosphere to be awkward around the table, but the kids chat as though one of us isn't going home today: exclamations of *so-and-so's tree was so cool* and endless questions about the fairies and magic to Bridgette, some of which she can answer and many she can't.

Perhaps they're all foolishly sure, like me, that someone else's tree was worse and so they must be safe.

Bridgette asks us all to stand once we've finished eating. She walks off into the kitchen without explanation, and the kids' cheery conversation rolls to a halt. Sierra grips the back of her chair. Timmy runs his hand across the back of his neck. Jemima smooths her hands down her skirt, and Brandon rocks slightly from side to side.

Bridgette returns with a tray of five porcelain teacups. Gold on the outside, white on the inside, and full of a steaming, opaque red liquid. She places each cup very deliberately in front of each of us, and then steps away from the table.

"At the bottom of each of these cups is a symbol. If you have a red circle underneath your tea, that means I am inviting you to stay another day. If you have a red cross there instead, you will be driving back with Carina this afternoon."

"Noughts and crosses," Sierra murmurs, and Bridgette smiles briefly.

The next five minutes or so stretches on like taffy. We stand in relative silence as our cups cool, taking tiny sips of sweet, cinnamon-flavoured tea, burning our lips and tongues, both eager and dreading the picture on the bottom.

Finally, my tea has reached a more acceptable temperature. I gulp down the remaining half with eyes squeezed shut, and then pop them open one at a time. Clearly visible through the last remnants of liquid and a smattering of tea leaves is a perfect, beautiful circle in foxtail red.

I look up. Sierra is smiling, her empty cup resting on the table. Jemima grins silently, cradling her cup to her chest. The boys are still finishing their tea. Brandon finally pulls his cup back with knitted brows, and then almost drops it on the tiled floor.

"What?" he says, and then makes an effort to lower his voice. "It's me?"

Bridgette puts a gentle hand on his shoulder. "I'm sorry, Brandon. Someone had to go. Grab your bag, please, and I'll take you down to the gate."

We wave Brandon off from the front porch. The remainder of the afternoon involves the children enjoying supervised chats to their parents from Bridgette's landline, some impromptu games of Four Square and Harry Potter themed Cluedo, and me wandering throughout the house and orchard for additional tree ideas.

As we're packing away the board games pieces, I ask the children why they applied for this competition when they still thought it was for a regular, non-magical orchard. With slightly hunched shoulders, Timmy says that his parents thought the land, and possibly the orchard itself, would be worth a lot of money.

Sierra nods in agreement. "And that 'Agrarian Ambassador' would look good on university applications."

"There might've been horses!" Jemima adds, and that her parents almost didn't let her come. They're now staying in a hotel nearby in case she needs them.

After dinner, Bridgette invites me to have a wine with her, if I haven't already planned to use that time for something else. I haven't.

We tuck ourselves into either end of the turquoise velvet couch. She swirls the red wine gently in her cup. "I really liked your application."

Oh, God. I hurry to swallow my mouthful. I'd always pictured the competition judges as a bespectacled panel of baby boomers and had stupidly not amended that picture after arriving here. Bridgette must be able to see me burning up.

"Oh," I manage. "I—You read it. Thank you."

"Tell me: you already have your own adult life back at home. Why would you want to drop everything to come here?"

I press myself back into the corner of the couch. "I don't really, though. I mean, I don't have a life," I amend. "I thought I would have one. What I do have now is a job that's going nowhere and no partner and no family. So not a lot to drop, really."

When I can bear to glance up, Bridgette's looking me right in the eyes and smiling softly, and somehow it only makes me feel a smidgen more embarrassed. "Well," she says, "I'm sorry things didn't work out as you planned. Life can be terribly unkind."

"It can." I pick up my wineglass again, even though I'm not keen on red wine, because it's comforting to hold. "I'm hoping new things will be better."

I watch her take another sip of wine. Study the delicate laugh lines around her eyes. The quirk of her mouth. The way her gloved hand cradles her glass.

"I'm glad you're here, Emily," she says.

Breath by breath, I feel my coiled muscles start to unwind. "I'm glad I'm here, too."

Bridgette retires to her bedroom soon after, and I stay on the couch smoothing the velvet under my bare feet. There's a faint imprint in the fibres from where Bridgette was sitting. If I look over my shoulder, I can see the waxing gibbous moon outside the glass door. And then someone stage whispers my name.

The cobalt-haired fairy half-flies, half-climbs up the couch leg and waves her tiny hand. She removes a detached fairy wing from where it's been tucked down the front of her tulle dress and scoots over to present it to me. "You can use this tomorrow."

My hand twitches towards it. "Isn't that cheating?"

"Why would it be? You're allowed to use something that's already here, with its owner's permission, and it's given freely."

I check to see if any of her wings are missing, but they all appear intact. Do fairies shed? I pinch the wing gently between my fingers, thin and fragile like cellophane. "Are you helping all of us?"

Her mouth contorts like she's trying not to laugh. "Hardly. We want you to stay. Bridgette likes you, we can tell." She winks, exaggerated so I can't miss it in the dim light.

"Likes me?"

"No harm in a little matchmaking." She pads over to the edge of the couch. "Use it," she demands, and flutters to the floor.

Because I can come up with no better plan and am slowly acknowledging that I *do* want to win, I plant the wing the following morning, having wrapped it carefully in my favourite sterling silver chain.

The tree that emerges resembles a futuristic office building, layers of metal floors divided by shiny, translucent walls clearly modelled after fairy wings. Tiny blue veins map the whole structure, and between every few floors pulses a white, fleshy sphere which immediately reminds me of a heart. Fairies much smaller than I'm used to swarm and disperse throughout the tree like harried bees.

We plant in the opposite order to yesterday, with Sierra first. She plants three tubes of her oil paints tied together with an elastic band, and the tree that emerges looks entirely made of paint, like it was plucked from a canvas and transformed to enormous 3D. You can see each individual brush stroke that composes it from roots to tip.

Jemima plants a masquerade mask, the kind that would cover the whole top half of her face if she wore the elastic. It looks like she's coloured it herself with primary school markers and paints. Its tree is a mass of tightly packed dirt with hundreds of masks dangling from the branches like overripe fruit. Masks of dozens of materials and in every possible shape. And from a couple of higher branches, I see what looks like a few masks made from human skin.

I don't quite see what Timmy's seeds are. They look like a miscellaneous mess cupped deep in his child hands. I ask him later and he says it was two eyes from an action figure and three twigs covered in chin blood. When his tree sprouts it seems to be an ordinary oak tree, the most ordinary tree in the orchard, but then its branches shiver and three slits open in its trunk: two large eyes that could have been transplanted from a giant doll, and a smiling gash of a wooden mouth trickling with sap and blood.

"Nice to meet you," growls Timmy's tree.

We sip the cinnamon tea from the porcelain teacups. My heart beats against my chest like a battering ram, and I have to sit down to finish so I don't spill anything.

I latch my eyes closed again to empty the cup. Before I can force myself to open them, Sierra says, "Oh!" like she's stepped on a Lego.

Over my own red circle, I spot her struggling to compose herself. "I, um, wasn't expecting that," she says. Pinpricks of tears are welling in the corners of her eyes. "You guys all did really good. Keep it up. Good luck with the rest of everything."

Bridgette takes Sierra's cup with care. "Your tree was really lovely, Sierra. I'm so glad it's part of the orchard."

Sierra's face reads *Not lovely enough*, but only for a moment. Then she's hugging Bridgette and the rest of us with what seems to be genuine affection and goes to collect her bag with dry eyes.

After dinner, Bridgette and I tuck ourselves back into the ends of the turquoise couch. I've declined another glass of wine, but Bridgette has one, and has a fire crackling in the nearby fireplace. Our socked toes touch in the middle of the couch. My feet are basking, euphoric, in the warmth of the flames and her body heat. Neither of us has moved them away.

"Aren't you worried they'll tell someone?" I say. "Brandon and Sierra, when they get back?"

"Oh no." Bridgette winks at me above her glass. "I have my tea."

It takes me a couple of seconds, but I say, "The red tea? With the noughts and crosses?"

She nods around a mouthful of wine. "If you have a cross, then your tea is a little different. By the time you reach the gate you'll have forgotten anything magic, anything fantastic about this place. It's just a regular orchard."

This knowledge drops inside me like a shotput. The loss. My hands come up to wrap around my neck like armour.

"I need my precautions," Bridgette continues. "Like the ribbon around the grounds. It's a ward so that no-one can see what this place really looks like, from the ground or from the air."

"Of course," I say, but the fire is much too hot now, like I'm going to burn right through the bottom of the couch. The living room is blurring, so I stare at my legs.

Bridgette's gloved hands come to rest on my shins. "Emily?"

"I'll forget all of this," I say, and am surprised at the emotion thick in my voice. "And it's…" *The most amazing thing to ever happen to me.* I take a pint-sized gasp of air. "Because I'm going to lose."

"Oh, Emily," she says, and again I'm surprised by the lack of judgement. "If I didn't think you could win, I wouldn't have invited you." She holds out her gloves, the firelight playing gently over the crimson leather. "Take off my gloves."

I scoot forward and pull the leather off her fingers one by one, a centimetre at a time, and hear my breath slow as I work. By the time I'm working my fingers under the cuffs, brushing my fingertips against her palms, my breathing is almost normal.

Bridgette places the gloves onto the coffee table. She leans forward and cups my cheeks with her hands. Her fingers are warm from the gloves and the fire, but the scars across her palms are still chilled. I shiver.

"Is this okay?" she asks.

"Yes," I say.

She uncurls her legs, and then picks mine up so they're stretched over her lap. "Is this okay?"

"Yes," I say.

She's closer and closer, and then she's kissing me. Her lips are softer than the turquoise velvet, softer than snakeskin. She smells of woodsmoke and cherries and mint. Her hand wraps around the back of my neck, warm outer and cold middle. The shotput has dislodged from my belly, and in its place my torso is filling with helium, my arms and legs are blooming with cherry blossoms.

I entwine my fingers with her free hand and break the kiss to breathe. "I, uh, don't want to win because of this."

She chuckles low in her throat. "Don't worry, you definitely won't." And Bridgette kisses me again.

She leaves me alone about ten minutes after, with swollen lips and half a glass of wine she's forgotten to finish. I carry it to the sink and let my fingertips flutter over the places she's touched me: cheeks, chin, lips, neck, waist, her legs under the back of my thighs.

I pour myself a glass of water. Once I'm feeling a little less heady, I turn my attention to finding a seed for tomorrow. I'm going to win, and I'm going to do it myself, without any more help. It's only ten to ten at night. There's still time.

I head back to my room and pick through every last one of my possessions, turning out the pockets for trinkets I could have missed, emptying my handbag on my bed, tossing out the contents of my suitcase. I amass a small collection of lint-covered coins, hair ties and USB drives loaded with years-old documents. I find a couple of receipts, to-do lists and start of a poem. Finally, running my hands around the inside walls of my suitcase, I feel something more promising.

I unzip the large pocket in the roof of my suitcase, the one I barely use as it's too thin to put more than a couple of t-shirts in and pull out a small wad of papers. My divorce papers, lodged in amongst some other identification documents. This particular copy looks very well-loved, all rubbed around the edges and smudged with ink where my tears sank into the paper. There's a grease stain from ramen noodles on pages 2-4. The bottom corners are all warped from the sweat of my right hand. The second-last page has a tiny streak of blood from a papercut.

I roll up the divorce papers like a runner's baton. A pleasant, low buzz of adrenaline courses through me.

This—this could be something amazing.

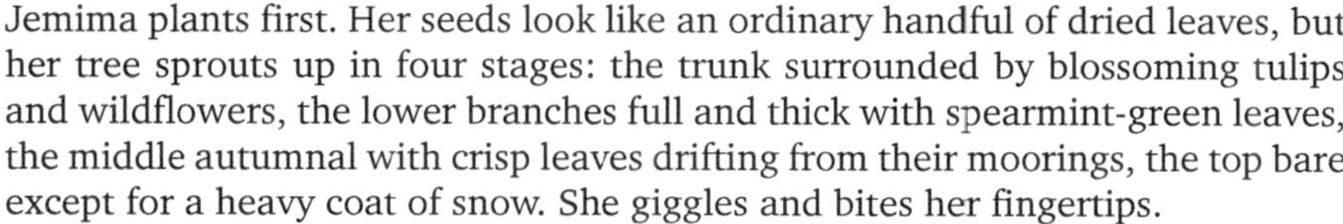

Jemima plants first. Her seeds look like an ordinary handful of dried leaves, but her tree sprouts up in four stages: the trunk surrounded by blossoming tulips and wildflowers, the lower branches full and thick with spearmint-green leaves, the middle autumnal with crisp leaves drifting from their moorings, the top bare except for a heavy coat of snow. She giggles and bites her fingertips.

Timmy buries a small gift box, shiny white with a candy-pink ribbon. His tree emerges fully covered in charcoal fur. A dozen bottle-green eyes blink at us from where they're sprinkled through its pelt, and tiny replicas of the gift box are tied with ribbons to the ends of several furry twigs. The wind blows one of them loose and Timmy hurries to collect it, but these new boxes are empty.

I kiss my rolled-up divorce papers before tucking them into their hole, feeling foolish and hopeful but mostly numb, which is usual for when I want something bad enough but may not get it. The tree shoots up like a swimmer desperate for air, short and thick with only a smattering of naked branches at the canopy, like a stout and leafless palm tree. Its trunk is covered in scabs where others would have bark, solid and layered and peeling. As we watch, some of the scabs fall away, leaving flickering pictures in the blood: people kneeling, weeping; slamming doors and suitcases; angry silhouettes curling into themselves—but also the joyful kneeling of proposals, comfortable embraces, kisses and gift giving. Before long, the images fade and the blood drips down, leaving only patches of perfect white paper in their place.

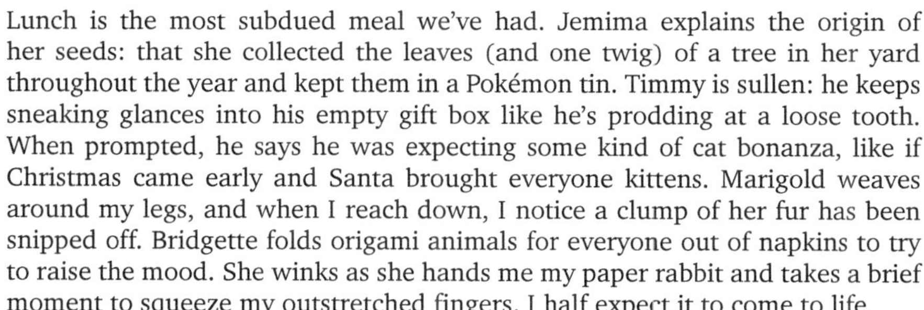

Lunch is the most subdued meal we've had. Jemima explains the origin of her seeds: that she collected the leaves (and one twig) of a tree in her yard throughout the year and kept them in a Pokémon tin. Timmy is sullen: he keeps sneaking glances into his empty gift box like he's prodding at a loose tooth. When prompted, he says he was expecting some kind of cat bonanza, like if Christmas came early and Santa brought everyone kittens. Marigold weaves around my legs, and when I reach down, I notice a clump of her fur has been snipped off. Bridgette folds origami animals for everyone out of napkins to try to raise the mood. She winks as she hands me my paper rabbit and takes a brief moment to squeeze my outstretched fingers. I half expect it to come to life.

We take our cinnamon tea like it's medicine. No-one seems to be rushing this time. I still finish first, eyes wide open this time, like if I keep watching it can't hurt me. And it's a big satisfying red nought that fills me all the way up.

When the others stop sipping, they're completely silent. Jemima and Timmy look straight at each other, put down their cups at the same time, identical wide-eyed pain on their faces. I'm hit with the unexpected thought that the competition might be over already—that they might both be going home.

But Jemima breaks their eye contact. "I'm sorry, Timmy," she says.

And Timmy musters a sad little smile. He nods at everyone and leaves without another word.

After Jemima has been tucked into bed, Bridgette and I head behind the house to moon watch. Underneath the filter of darkness, the back garden still shimmers where moonlight glances off beetles and koi, or where fireflies swirl between pockets of fern fronds. We settle on a pair of wrought iron chairs, and Bridgette explains how she inherited the orchard from her grandmother, who knew of its magical potential but had chosen to opt out. When Bridgette moved in, there had been a single otherworldly tree hidden within wooden stakes, connected by a square of black ribbon.

When she's finished her story, Bridgette unhinges a rectangular metal tin decorated with Van Gogh's *The Starry Night*. There are several white lumps inside, all glossy with icing. "Take a bite," she offers. "But promise you won't let go of my arm."

She probably can't see my quirked eyebrow in the darkness. I take a solid grip on her lower arm and sink my teeth into one of the desserts. It tastes like marzipan, like coffee cream, like popping candy. The popping sensation spreads down my body like a wave; a bubbling, a fizzing, a lightness. I drop the half-eaten iced lump onto the iron table. I can no longer feel the metal of the chair against my legs. I am rising. I am floating in the air like a helium balloon, anchored to Bridgette like her arm has my string.

Bridgette laughs with joy and swallows a mouthful of her own dessert. She rises up to meet me like it's effortless, and we float higher and higher, until we're just above the garden, until we're level with the first storey roof. I gaze at Bridgette, wide-eyed, but she only looks blissful.

"This is what I wanted to show you!" she calls, louder than necessary given we're clutching each other's forearms. "Do you like it? It's perfectly safe, I promise; we won't get much higher, and we'll drop down again after about twenty minutes. But isn't it fun?"

I am overcome. A light wind is pushing us slowly away from the house, so I can see all of the back garden from the air and much of the orchard stretching out before us. Bridgette is smiling at me, so wide and so affectionate. I feel the freedom of weightlessness, like being suspended in the middle of a swimming pool. And in a sudden, uncontrollable rush I start to weep, and can hear it as a thick waver in my voice.

"I love it," I say. "It's the best thing ever. But I don't want to lose it tomorrow."

Bridgette isn't smiling anymore. "You keep talking about what you don't want," she says. "Stop. Tell me what you *do* want."

"I..." I squeeze the flesh of her arm until it hurts my hand. I feel like I'm about to be sucked into space. "I want to win the competition. I want to look after the orchard. Plant things in it. I want to stay. I want to stay here with you. I want to *be*... with you."

I force myself to look at her. It's hard to read Bridgette's expression in the dark, but she's nodding. "Thank you," she says gently. "That means so much to me."

I wipe at my eyes with my free hand.

"Please try to enjoy yourself."

And I take a couple of minutes to recover, but we're *flying*, and it's beautiful, and then I laugh and don't know why.

I plant our two half-eaten desserts. I expect the tree to be somehow symbolic of our affection, of hope, some kind of mixture of our saliva—something charming and romantic. What sprouts is a gorgeous, leafless giant, trunk and branches all made of hardened icing with a hill of powdered sugar around the base. It's lovely in its simplicity, but it's far too simple. Even when the tree disconnects from the soil and levitates above the powdered sugar hill, roots swaying in the breeze, I know it won't be enough to win.

Jemima has come to the final planting empty-handed. When Bridgette asks her about it, she says she has her seed inside her shoes. And she wants my help with getting it out. I am a little stunned but have no reason to refuse. I follow her to the patch of grass which will be the competition's last planting site.

Instead of crouching like we usually do, Jemima sits firmly on the grass. She takes off one buckled leather shoe, and one frilly white sock, and I peer inside them for secrets, but they appear to be empty. I don't understand how I'm expected to help. And then Jemima removes the whole lower half of her left leg and holds its skin-coloured plastic straight up to make sure I've seen. Underneath her skirt, her flesh-and-blood leg finishes just above the knee.

As she scoops out a hole large enough for her prosthetic leg, I ask, "Are you sure you want to use that?"

"I'm sure," she says. "I have a spare in my bag back at the house. I just need you to pull me to safety, please."

I nod vacantly. I have been beaten fairly by a child a third my age. When she finishes planting, I grab her swiftly under the arms, scooping her away from her winning tree, with neither of us acquiring so much as a scratch.

Bridgette escorts me down towards the bottom of the hill. I have dutifully drunk the awful tea. I try to tie the memories of magic around my mind like strings around my fingers, but I know they will come undone. I have written several notes to myself with Sierra's old sharpie, scrawled across my stomach underneath my breasts. They will probably read like words penned while half asleep in the earliest hours of the morning. I will not understand. Magic evaporates in the daytime. Magic loses its power against the bleakness of the everyday.

But I do not want to steep in such a black mood for Bridgette's final goodbye. I try to shrug off some of my heaviness and concentrate on her hand in mine. That, I should still remember. She's taken off one of her gloves, where she's holding me, and her skin is both soft and corded, warm and chilling from her scarring. The unworn glove pokes out of her breast pocket like a corsage.

I study the vibrancy of the grass, peppered with tiny daisies, and the solidity of the trees flanking the wrought iron gate. The sun bathes us in perfect light, and within moments my dark mood seems to fall away like an old skin. Why on earth should I mourn the loss of a fruit orchard that I never really wanted? If anything, surely the loss is—

"Listen," I say, pausing about twenty paces to the gate. "I can barely keep a cactus alive. I don't know why I thought I would be any good with an orchard. But I have so enjoyed meeting you. Perhaps, even though I didn't win, you might like to join me for dinner sometime? I could maybe come back down here in a couple of weeks?"

I've never seen Bridgette caught off guard before, and feel immediately anxious that I've said something wrong, that she's going to take her hand away…

"You don't want the orchard anymore," she says, in a monotone, "but you still want me?"

I am struck with paralysis, unsure of exactly how I've screwed this up. Have I offended her beloved orchard? Does she see me as inconsistent and unreliable, guilty of wasting her time? "Yes," I manage, but my voice is too high. "Jemima will be better with the orchard. I have a brown thumb. But I still think you're wonderful."

Her eyes gradually curl up at their edges again, and finally Bridgette is looking at me with all of the affection I could wish for. "I'd like that. Please do visit again soon. Carina will let you in."

And then she is kissing me in the middle of the field, one gloved hand and one bare against my cheeks, and I can feel the glorious curves and bones of her pressed against my torso through her dress.

Bridgette takes a moment to recover her breath when she breaks away. "There may be some surprises when you come back."

"I can handle them."

She winks in reply, almost imperceptibly. "I know you can."

I take my paces backwards towards the gate. This is only a temporary parting. She looks at me as if I'm magic.

The Godhunter

Featured in Issue #77

...Evan Kennedy

It's a Tuesday at three in the afternoon when the Godhunter knocks on my door and says "I'm going to kill them all."

"Witness protection my ass," I quip. I try for a dry chuckle, but it comes out in a rattle, so I take another drink of my Miller Light and let him in. He glances around my trailer for a place to sit, then just stands there toeing the cracked linoleum with his hands on his hips.

I glance at him as I get another beer, trying to stop my hands from trembling. "Mack gave you my name, I guess?"

"This is a high priority in Washington," he says, steepling his fingers. "Agent McElroy was very accommodating." In my head this is where he's supposed to light a cigarette, but he doesn't. There are no nicotine stains on his fingers and no alcohol on his breath. It throws me off. I always pictured government assassins being a little more hard-boiled. Rough around the edges. This guy looks like a boy scout.

A boy scout in a three-piece suit who kills gods. I've seen weirder, I guess.

I say, "You're the one who assassinated Hekaih. And the Oaken."

"You've heard of me."

I can't tell if he's pleased. He still has his sunglasses on. Indoors. "And you're the cultist who turned state's evidence on all those transmortals. Your testimony led to the *Leavitt Media Act*."

Time was, you could turn on the TV and see a god on every channel. But I convinced the House Transmortal Affairs Committee that Old Ones feed on fame. So nowadays, you so much as tweet about a god and you get an unpleasant visit from the suits. *And how shall they believe in him of whom they have not heard?* Done and done. God Bless America.

"I don't want any part of this," I say, because already I'm having visions of bleeding skies and some cowardly part of me wishes he'd go away so I could get back to getting drunk. The nighthooks will be bad tonight, even with my dream-worm in.

"You have a comfortable place here," he says, running a dubious finger through the dust on my microwave. "It can either continue to be comfortable, or…" He lets the threat hang in the air, ugly motes of word-poison dancing like dust in sunbeams. I fight down the urge to hold my breath.

I wrap my arms around myself, shrinking into my chair. "You can't kill them. They'll know. You have *no idea* what they'll do to you. To both of us. You're probably killing me just by *being* here."

He doesn't flinch. "I came because I need your help. The government can no longer ignore the threat transmortal entities pose to national security. And you know more about them than any man alive."

"I'm an apostate. I'm not involved with the gods anymore," I tell him. I can feel tears welling up in my eyes, but looking at him now—impassive behind those sunglasses—I know they won't help, knowing the way you taste danger in the place behind your heart.

"Well, to be frank," he drawls. "I'm not asking. I'm *telling*."

I force myself to take a breath; I expected this. "What do you need to know? Can we make it quick?"

A smile lurks at the corner of his mouth. "You misunderstand, Mr Temple. You're coming with me."

We're three rest-stops through Georgia before the Godhunter asks me about my first god.

I didn't expect Valkyrie hymns and busty bar-wenches, but I thought a cross-country *Götterdämmerung* would at least rate some spy gear and black helicopters. Instead I shove some talismans into a ratty backpack and bundle into the Godhunter's old Crown Victoria. He wants to kill them chronologically. So we're going to Florida.

"Why do you want to know?" I'm tasting the shape of plotlines by now, feeling the Godhunter's mind expand to fill his container, and I'm beginning to see myself through his eyes. Still, I'm sulking. It's true that this is my last, best chance at getting some closure. But it would have been polite of him to give me a choice.

His sunglassed eyes don't leave the road as he takes one last slurp of his Diet Coke. The straw makes a hollow noise like bones in chain.

"I need to know everything," he says. "I have to get inside their minds. Become One. That's the only way to do it. You have to let them into your heart, become like one of the devout. Love them. *Then* you can kill them." He looks over at me finally. "I gather you did."

"Kill them?" I swallow, feeling off balance. I expected a thug, but it's becoming clear that the Godhunter fancies himself some kind of great sage, equal to heaven.

"Love them," he says.

There is a long pause. Then I say, "It's easy to love Naya."

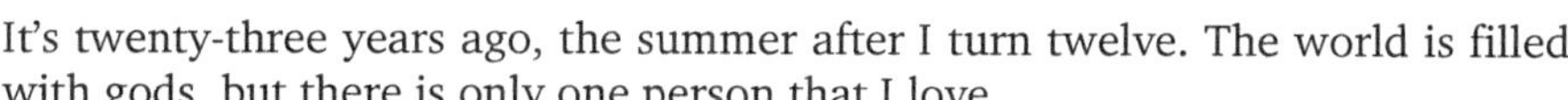

It's twenty-three years ago, the summer after I turn twelve. The world is filled with gods, but there is only one person that I love.

Mama cleans the Slushee machines at the 7/11 to feed me and my sister, Lizzie. She must be stressed, but she never lets us see it. She tells us that life is a journey, and that the bumpy road doesn't matter so long as you know where you're going. It is always best, she says, to have faith.

My father is a different story. When he's not driving for Schneider, his hobbies include drinking on the old thrift-store sofa, yelling at the TV, and slapping mama around. One day, he gets too drunk and bounces her head off the corner of the coffee table. I remember thinking that I didn't know there was that much blood in a human body.

When the cops and the social workers and the guidance counsellor at school tell me that I couldn't have known—that I was just a kid—I stop listening. They don't know what I saw, or what I felt.

Yeah, I was only twelve. But I could have told someone.

That's why I fall in love with the goddess Nayaserida. She takes me into her bosom and lets me cry by her sacred fire, and doesn't try to tell me it wasn't my fault.

She also tells me that I can fix it.

"I know this part," the Godhunter says. "She lent you the power of the Hearth to resurrect your mother. And it worked, if I'm not mistaken. For a while." He sucks on his Coke again. It must be mostly water by now.

"How long before you realised it wasn't really her?"

I cross my arms, angling my body away from him in the bucket seat. The scrabbling panic I felt when this man first darkened the kitchen of my double-wide is fading now, replaced by a kind of numbness, but I'm still fighting the urge to hide.

"Six months," I say. "Six months Naya drove Mama's body around like a puppet." It's been twelve years, now, and I can still see the blood streaming down my mother's empty face. "Naya didn't see any difference."

But the Godhunter doesn't ask about how I killed my mother the second time. Instead he shrugs and says "You were just a kid."

I wonder, not for the last time, whether he realises how unhelpful he is.

"The thing is," I say. "Naya wasn't even angry. She was just sad. Confused. She wanted me to stay, even after… everything." I shake my head. "She still wanted me."

The Godhunter's smile crawls out. "Good to know."

Family reunions are always awkward, and it's worse when your last parting involved a fire axe. I rub my palms on my thighs, trying and failing to keep from sweating in the oppressive Okefenokee heat.

O! My Darling Son! says Naya, and her voice is a warm blanket on my heart. *My Long-Lost One! My Son Is Returned!*

"It's true," I lie. "I'm home."

My smile feels a thousand watts of fake, but she doesn't notice. Everything about Nayaserida is so guileless, she has a hard time seeing deception in others. All I have to do is open my arms and she takes me into herself. When the Godhunter's deovenin gets into her system, she doesn't understand. She looks confused when the veins stand out black on her emerald skin, and even as she shifts through endless forms, she dies without changing expression.

When it's done, I spend a few moments standing over the dead crocodile who helped raise me as the Godhunter's soulcap drains the immanence from her body. Then I say, "You're not my mother. My mother is dead."

The Godhunter is standing beside me, then. When I turn to him, still wiping at tears, he gives my shoulder a squeeze that I find somewhat less avuncular than he probably intends. I've been seduced by far better creatures than he. "Good kill," he says. "Didn't think you had the stones."

"So what happened next?" the Godhunter asks. I-40 across Arkansas is empty enough that you have to keep busy or you go crazy. So I tell him about Mr Ash.

It's twenty-one years ago, and my mother has been dead for two years. A lot of fourteen-year-olds are angry, but I'm a special case. The Godhunter has read my file, so he knows about the drugs and the shoplifting and the fire-starting that got me tossed back by three different foster families. But he doesn't know how I got Carl and Janet Temple to stick with me for three whole years.

Mr Ash is a stormlord, one of the two-faced gods. Sometimes he's making crops grow, and sometimes he's whipping up tornadoes.

"Ash is capricious," I say. "But he's also smart. There's a method to it."

"He taught you how to do it. He Masked you."

I shrug. "Standard Jekyll-and-Hyde. I kept my nose clean for Carl and Janet, and at night I went out and did whatever I wanted."

"But then you started splitting." The Godhunter has done his homework. He has all the lingo dead, dry, and pinned under glass.

There's a long pause, then I say, "The Temples were good people. They deserved better than me. That's why I used their name for witness protection. I wanted to see if I could be a normal person. Like them."

"You said 'me,'" the Godhunter observes. "Wasn't that your Hyde half?"

"That's not how splitting works," I say. "Both parts are still you. Or… I dunno, maybe neither one is. It just warps your perspective. Affects how you think."

"If you seek to be pardoned from your sins," he says, "You must give up credit for your virtues as well." His eyes are unreadable behind the dark glasses, but his smile stalks me from tall grass.

I think Mr Ash is glaring at me, but it's hard to tell because he has a thunderstorm where the top half of his head should be.

Breakups are hard.

You Crawl Half-Hearted To Myself For Penance, his voice thunders in my head. *You Of The Re-Mingled Mind! You Who Once Saw Hot And Crimson! Life Pulsed In Your Hands, Calling You Master! You Are Apostate! You Should Be Charred! Drowned! Broken!*

"You speak truly, my Lord." I don't look up as I talk, my breath making whorls in the dust. "Unmake me if that is thy will." It's scary, but I've been practicing this in the mirror back at the Motel 6, and it does the trick. When Mr Ash lifts my head, his face is blue skies and a summer that never ends.

You Had Such Promise. You Knew The Height Of Mercy And The Depth Of Peace. You've Turned Now To All The Prettiest Heresies. You Are Become Less Than You Were. Do You Remember What It Was To Know Reason And To Know Madness?

"I want to be that again," I say. "To be like you."

He lifts me from the Oklahoma clay, then, and leads me to his inner chambers and sends away his retainers. We talk for what seems like a lifetime, but it's really only about thirty minutes before the change comes. One minute he's robed in the sky and clothed with the evening clouds, and the next minute he is become One again, and I know the Godhunter has finished breaking into the compound and destroying the phylactery that holds Ash's soul.

Mr Ash tries to fight back, but without his immanence he's just this skinny old man, and I can see his eyes. I shoot him twice in the chest, then once in the head just to make sure. I can tell the Godhunter is parked outside because Ash's essence flows through the window in a steady stream, caught in the soulcap in the trunk of the Crown Vic, but by the time I come outside he's already gone.

When I make it back to the hotel, the Godhunter is channel-surfing. "Thanks for waiting on me," I snap.

The Godhunter is immune to sarcasm. "The phylactery was right where you said. And you were just the distraction. The unbinding spell was the hard part." He doesn't look away from the celebrity cooking competition on the TV. I wonder how he can see it through his dark glasses. "You did just fine cleaning up what was left. I was ready to jump in if you lost your nerve. Wanted to watch you do it."

I take a long breath. Then I say, "You can't just hide the evil parts of yourself. You have to kill them."

"Profound insight," he says. "Does it make you feel better about torturing

Carl and Janet's Shih Tzu to death?"

"Get bent," I say, then I go to bed.

It's eighteen years ago, and I'm just young enough to not get tried as an adult. Seventeen year-olds aren't cute anymore, and animal cruelty is a felony in Oklahoma. I spend six months in juvie, then a buddy gets me a job at a lumber company in the northwest.

In the car on the way to Oregon, I tell the Godhunter about meeting Lilit among the towering redwoods, about how her owl eyes fixed me in the darkness and her forked tongue tasted my lips. I don't give any specific details about the best sex of my life, but the Godhunter already has Lilit pegged as an easy mark. All I have to do is to get back into her bed.

After the Godhunter plunges the thrice-bless'd kukri dagger into Lilit's back during the heat of passion wherein she gives up her utter self, I say "Listen, why do you even need me?"

"How's that?" he asks, swabbing the ichor from the crude logographs on the carved-bone blade.

I stand listless, drawing in ragged breaths and looking down at the godsblood matting my chest hair. The woman who took my virginity is considerably less attractive in death, all mottled scales and twisted feathers, and I'm already getting cold, the way you do when your gods die.

"I'm not really helping. You already know these things. I'm just the bait." My voice trembles, and I hate myself for it. "Anyone could do that."

The Godhunter tips his chin at the bed. "You don't think this one deserved it."

I glossed over some details in this case because I knew he would scoff. Infidelity isn't exactly surprising from a sex goddess. But not everyone walks in on their first love having an orgy with their logging crew.

"I don't want to do this anymore. I'm scared and I hate this. *Please* let me go home."

He coaxes the knife back into its sheath, murmuring Amharic nothings. The grey glow fades and we both breathe again. "Don't get cold feet on me now," he says. "She stirred up your head with her mystical juju, made you not yourself."

"That's what love means," I say, trying it out, seeing if I believe it. "It was my fault. I wanted her to be something she wasn't. Wanted her to complete me. But she couldn't. None of them could."

The Godhunter rolls his eyes behind the dark glasses. "She's not human, Temple. She was a monster. And she didn't love you back. She was just using you."

"Yeah," I say. "It's just..."

"I get it. It's just 'cuz she was your first." He pushes past me. "Do what the rest of us do and go get laid."

They start to blur together after a while. I'm granted passage to The Bha'o'mot's underwater kingdom in the bay off of Tijuana, where I pry open the Hlaare Clam to reveal the piercing voice of the jet-black pearl within, and my gill scars burn as his corpse rots on the beach. My sister Lizzie's body floats to the surface. For some reason she's kept aging even though she's been dead for fifteen years, ever since I convinced her to join the pod. I can't bring myself to bury her, so she stays on the beach alongside the great leviathan. I don't tell the Godhunter who she is, but by now I can feel his smirk crawling up my back.

We carve the scaly wings from Most-Sensitive-Yanlun and cast him from his Rocky Mountain aerie, poison the wells of Fontus Deepseer in Arizona, and catch Nañsî'inLak the Fox in his own traps. I shed the sister-soul that's been swirling in the whalebone prison of my false elbow, the scales fall from my back, my left eye turns from shrill viridian to brown and shrinks back to its normal size, and I stop tasting the sensation of being lost in a prehistoric forest on the back of my tongue. The soulcap in the trunk of the Crown Vic swells atrociously and suspires in time with some faraway lung. Still we press on, always and ever to the next fresh god.

Every time I amputate a love from my heart and leave it bloody in a hotel dumpster, I grow a little thinner, plucked and measured by wrinkled claws, clucked over by disapproving tongues. The Godhunter sees that I will fade away and return not to dust but to void, I am certain, and there will be naught whatever to mark my passage. The Godhunter tells me that I will feel better the more that I kill, but instead I only feel more afraid.

He is getting everything he wanted, and he doesn't even have the grace to act pleased.

"Hey! Are you listening? What's wrong with you?"

I turn in my seat, hugging my knees to my chest. I'm trying to stop shaking. It's a long way from Nañsî'inLak's California burrow to upstate New York, and since the Godhunter always drives I have claimed dominion over the passenger side of the Crown Victoria.

I have never been anywhere but here, I know now. I am Manuhala, the great bird, whose hunger shall consume the world. I have nested here in this cracked upholstery, moulting coffee cups and candy bar wrappers, keeping my belly filled against that day. My body says all this and more, while my mouth lies. It has always been thus between the Godhunter and I, and I can no longer tell which part of me lies and which part speaks the truth.

I say, "Huh?"

"You can't crap out on me now. We're here! It's almost over!" The Godhunter slurps his third can of Red Bull hollow, his head thrown back to the sky. He hasn't slept in 36 hours.

I feel as if the soulcap in the back of the car is taking parts of myself along with my gods. The Godhunter doesn't say he believes this too, but I see through his eyes. He knows how these things work. He read my file.

He also knows that I threw away my dream-worm at a rest stop in Missouri. My nighthooks are gone. I sleep now like the dead man that I am.

"We're here and you still haven't told me about Father," he says, leaning into the car through the driver's side window. "Is there anything I might need to know?"

I shake my head, noticing where we are, at last. "I... I dunno." The lilac trees fill my vision through the car's windshield. Their smell fills my hands and spills through my fingers, and I taste home on my tongue.

"You don't know? What the hell kind of answer is that?" His finger snaps are like gunshots in the claustrophobic sedan. "Wake up, Temple!"

So I tell him what I must.

It's five years ago and I am so, so tired. I've been used and scarred and broken and betrayed. Being big and old and powerful is practically against the law now, thanks to me. But I hear about the Father who lives in the lilac grove in upstate New York and I tell myself, *just one more.*

One last god.

The things that happen to you when you're young, they shape you, I tell the Godhunter. Your model for what a relationship should be gets weird and you get in this cycle where you just keep picking people who are bad for you—sniffing out new pieties, hunting down new abusers—because it's the only thing you know how to do. But eventually, if you're very, very lucky, you meet someone different.

All my life I have been what others saw in me. Naya needed to be a perfect mother. Mr Ash needed to corrupt so he could save. Lilit needed to be flattered. On and on and on, I became what they needed. Soldier or tool, companion or lover, strong or weak, quiet or loud, sweet or cruel. I had so many gods that there was nothing left of me, if I ever existed at all. I was each of them entire to myself, gave them everything I could be, and when they were gone, nothing beside remained. I believed for so long that I was only worth what someone else saw in me and I never found someone who could tell me who I truly am.

But Father tells me to go away. He tells me, so gently, that before I can try to please someone else I must first be satisfied in myself. That I must know where I'm going before I can decide who to follow.

He doesn't want to be worshipped.

Father shows me that there is a person inside me, a real person, and that it's a person who can be found. I have been dead, but I can live again.

But more than that, Father is the first one to ask what I want. So I tell him the truth.

I don't want it to ever happen to anyone else.

I want them to be finished. Every god, every titan, every old and preening thing latched wormlike in my heart. I want them dead. And I want to be the one to do it.

The Godhunter is rushed, and sloppy. Has he pushed me too hard, he wonders? Used me too much? Will the power be enough for his ascension? Will he have the strength of all the gods, or will he find himself stuck, half-hearted, no longer a man but not quite divine?

This is what he wants, I know. I've always known. The motives for deicide are few, undertaken only for love or for envy, and the Godhunter was never one to bend the knee.

I ask him, and he's too distracted even to lie with his mouth. Father has come upon us, and even now the figure in white moves amongst the lilac trees.

"You're done, Temple. Just relax. This will be all the power I need." He raises the godgun, the massive rifle with the three black-stone bullets he's been saving for just this moment. He removes his sunglasses, and his smirk springs its claws. "You've been very helpful. I may even let you live."

I see now fully the redness of the light in his eyes, so I give him the answer I've been holding at the centre of my heart. "I remember more," I say. He's not paying attention. But I tell him anyway.

It's three weeks ago, the Monday night before the Godhunter visits me for the very first time, and it's dark in my trailer, and cramped, but when Father comes to me he fills the house with light.

The one we spoke of is on his way, he tells me. *Even now he has struck down Hekaiah, and The Oaken. The dark ones are weakened by lack of belief, and now they will perish at his hand. When he comes to you, you must go with him. He will help you. Dark are his designs, but he knows not that he does the work of the Light, and all his striving will not avail him. Your time is almost complete, my old friend.*

"I'm so frightened," I tell him. "What if I don't have the strength?"

He kisses my forehead and dries my tears. *I will be with you*, he says.

I love you.

The Godhunter has put a bullet into Father's right shoulder, and so it takes him a moment to process what I've been saying. When he does, it's already too late.

While I'm talking, I snatch the keys from the ignition and bail out the passenger side, crouching low as I dash to the trunk. He lets out a cry and swings his rifle around. I throw up the trunk lid, and the Godhunter's second bullet punches through the aluminium, throwing the shot wild in a puff of insulation and slamming the lid down onto my shoulder. I feel my collar bone snap, and lights burst behind my eyes. When I can see again, I'm lying on my back in the grass. The Godhunter is screaming my name, rage boiling under his tongue, and he raises the rifle to put his third and final shot between my eyes, but suddenly Father is there, and before I can stop it he throws himself between us.

The Godhunter curses aloud as Father collapses, and fumbles to turn the gun around. He lifts the rifle butt to crush and scatter me under the lilac trees, but from the ruin of the trunk I can see the soulcap throbbing, sensing its time is nigh at hand. It glows with a terrible red light, but in the end it's a fragile thing, made from faery dreams and spun sugar and subcutaneous tissue, and the plain old regular bullets in the spare pistol I took from under the driver's seat tear it asunder like the real world through a dream.

At the first crack of the pistol the Godhunter doubles over, at the second he vomits in the grass, and at the third something breaks in him and he slumps. The world is receding through fog and my shoulder burns with hate, but I keep firing until the pistol clicks and clicks and the red light fades from the Godhunter's eyes.

Once I'm sure it's finished, I drag myself back to where Father is lying in the grass. I choke off a sob as I see the godsblood pooling around him, and I pull his head into my lap. He smiles up at me and calls me friend.

"I tried," I say, feeling the tears come in earnest now. "I failed you. I'm so sorry."

His brow creases, and he reaches up to touch my cheek. He tells me that I haven't failed, and cannot fail, that nothing happens which should not.

This is love, he tells me. *Not to be served, but to serve.*

He shows me these things and more besides, and I become more than I was as I sit under the falling blossoms cradling the body of one who loves me.

When Father passes on, I have enough time to move away before the lilac tree grows from his body, taller and more magnificent than any the world has ever seen. I dry my tears, feeling cold the way you do when your gods die, but strong as well, stronger than I've been for as long as memory, despite my fractured shoulder. Bundling myself into the car is difficult with only one working arm, but I manage, and the keys are only a little bent from their adventure in the trunk. It takes a few tries to get the car started, but eventually it comes, as all things will.

The man who hunted for gods I leave buried under the lilac trees, and I drive away without looking back. The hardest part of the drive is working the blinker with only one hand, but I take it slow and everything goes fine. There is no need to rush once you know where you're going.

The Etiquette of Mythique Fine Dining

Featured in Issue #75

...Carolyn Rahaman

The protestors are the same crew as yesterday and the day before. Ava doesn't know any of their names, of course. She doesn't know what happened in their pasts to make them so energised about keeping people from eating the food at Mythique, so wound up with vengeance as to embarrass people every single morning as they walk to work. She knows them by face, by their outerwear that doesn't change. The signs they hold don't change day in and day out. There's the "MAGICAL BLOOD DOESN'T WASH OFF" sign and the "THERE'S SO LITTLE MAGIC IN THE WORLD" sign held by a pair who Ava imagines are married and retired and have a couple cats. There's the picture of the unicorn leg, which is supposed to be grisly, but Ava can't get over the fine marbling of the meat. There's the "MEAT IS MURDER" sign, which seems slightly off-message, but the other protestors don't seem to mind.

Their signs are lowered when Ava arrives. Someone has brought two carriers of coffee, and they're passing them around. Although they'll shout at anyone who uses the front door, the protestors don't start chanting until either Chef Augustine or Hampton, the general manager, arrive, and they disband shortly thereafter. Chef Augustine spends his early mornings at the fish and produce markets and won't arrive for another hour or so. They don't seem to realise that there's a back entrance that the rest of the chefs and the wait staff use. Maybe they don't realise there's more staff.

One of the protestors smiles at her and offers a mitten-clad wave. They see Ava every day, after all. They must think she works in the next building over.

She smiles back as she passes and turns into the alley. She's not afraid of the protestors.

She won't admit she's afraid of the kitchen.

In the break room, she strips off her coat and closes her eyes for a series of deep breaths before tying on her apron. Once she knots it, she'll be a cog in a machine, a tool that follows orders and cooks and sweats and does not talk back and takes it and takes it, *Yes, chef,* because she's learning, by God, one day she'll learn. She has to be stone, she has to be rock, because rocks don't cry. Chefs

45

don't cry.

She pulls her apron tight. Knots it in front, in back, and folds the top over the strings.

She lifts her chin. She has to be stone.

At Ava's interview, Chef Augustine asked her to make an omelette. She made it perfectly, deftly cracking and whisking eggs and milk in a glass bowl, *whisk whisk whisk whisk*. She slid butter around a pan and poured in the eggs before the butter pat finished melting. A couple quick nudges with a spatula, pulling the eggs towards centre, forming little wrinkles through which runny yolks flowed. A sprinkle of salt, a line of cheese, a flip with the spatula, a twist of the pan, and the omelette flipped onto the plate. Her heart swelled at the sight of it—fluffy, golden, and perfectly wrapped. Chef Augustine had nodded, taken a bite, and nodded again as he chewed with sharp, quick bites.

Still chewing, he said, "Good." He swallowed. "You start tomorrow."

"Yes, chef."

He pointed a finger at her, tossing the plate back onto the counter. "You're gonna hate it."

"No, chef."

"That's the last time you get to say that."

"Yes, chef."

She didn't hate it. She didn't hate it. She didn't hate it.

But that was a chicken egg omelette. That was before. Now she's in a whole new world.

Dennis, the *sous* chef, organises the unpacking of a delivery truck, laughing with one of the supplier guys as he signs off on a clipboard, and barking at the *commis* chefs as they heft bags of flour over their shoulders. Zach, the other greenhorn and only friend she has here, grabs her by the shoulders and herds her towards the truck as if he's a sheepdog. "Today's the day," he says. He nods at a violently blue crate of eggs, as if she doesn't know what he means. He lifts a foot onto the truck's running board to balance the crate on his bent knee, bouncing the crate once in his grip.

"Let's hope so," Ava says, tugging forward a crate of olive oil.

They hand everything off to Elisabetta, the *garde* manager, who's in a tizzy with a clipboard, moving back and forth, back and forth in the small space of the pantry, checking off a list and shifting crates a few inches to either side for reasons only fathomable to her. She has a pencil behind her ear and one in her hand.

Zach bounces on his toes. His T-shirt is as thin as it can be to still qualify as a shirt.

"You ready?" he asks.

Ava rolls her shoulders. She doesn't feel ready but says, "Always."

Zach shouts, "Dennis!"

Dennis looks up from his clipboard and his discussion with the *saucier*, annoyed for a second, then waves Zach and Ava on and goes back to his business.

Ava and Zach dig into the blue crate, not yet put away, and select three eggs each. Golden eggs from golden geese in Wisconsin, eggs that remind Ava of crafty Easter displays. Mythique doesn't use chicken eggs, and Ava isn't allowed to use any magical ingredients at all until she can prove herself by making a golden omelette just as perfect as a chicken egg omelette. Until then, she and Zach are stuck peeling potatoes and washing lettuce.

She's been trying for two weeks. Zach's been trying for three.

The burner flares. She cracks the eggs. At first glance, they're normal, the yolks a deep orange, but as she whisks (always counter-clockwise or it would froth into messy, lacy bubbles) light blooms from the glass bowl. She whisks to a specific tempo, with a specific beat that stutters, trips on every fifth beat. She bounces to the rhythm, and strictly does not look at Zach, who is also bouncing but doing his stutter-step off-time with her. Golden flecks pop in the mixture, rising then whisked away, startling her every time into thinking she's cracked some shell into it, but she doesn't falter, *whisk whisk whi-isk whisk whisk*. It has to be a light touch. Too hard and the golden sheen dulls. Butter in the pan, pour in the eggs, again in a counter-clockwise motion that feels wrong to her wrist. The eggs cook too fast, spitting and sizzling, tiny flecks of gold spewing up to singe her hands, the sight of which can be distracting. The spatula movements must come faster, but gentler—rippling the eggs, counter-clockwise again, and she's so close, she's almost got it, it's supposed to be runny, it's fine, *it's fine*. She grabs for the cheese and her hand smacks against the side of the bowl and wobbles and she panics, losing her cool for just a moment, but long enough. The omelette's burnt before she spreads the line of cheese, and she flips it onto the plate too fast, trying to make it before the golden hue vanishes in one final sputter.

It comes unfolded, and—as if the egg molecules can't exist in an imperfect state—they separate. The omelette reverts to a runny splat on a plate. There is no glowing.

Ava swears, wipes her hands on her apron. Five minutes in the kitchen, and she's already sweating.

A second later Zach groans. He claws fingers through his short hair and then covers his face as if he can hide from his shame. His omelette isn't liquid, but it looks like burnt toast in an awkward trapezoid shape.

Dennis leans over Zach's plate with a curve to his lip, then dumps the contents into the trash and tosses the plate back to the counter with a clatter. He makes a derisive, wet sound in the back of his throat at Ava's attempt. "Where did you apprentice?"

"Savant, chef."

No matter how much the back of her neck tingles, she holds firm as he moves closer into her space. She has to be rock. She has to be stone.

"If I call the Savant right now, would Chef Triallis answer or would I get your best friend Chrissy?"

"Chef Triallis, chef."

"You sure about that?"

"Yes, chef."

"Because Chef Triallis wouldn't put up with this shit. And that makes me think that the only explanation is that you lied on your résumé. That you're a fraud. Are you a fraud?"

"No, chef."

He picks up the plate, pressing it right under her nose. "I wouldn't ask the rats in the dumpster to eat this. Would you eat this?"

"No, chef."

"You will if I tell you to," he says. He presses closer. "Eat it."

She won't. She can't. She won't be humiliated.

She has to.

"Eat. It. This is what you're offering me. Eat it."

She doesn't know how to eat it. They had a fork ready, shining on the counter in hopes that it would get used for at least one of their omelettes. But the fork won't work. A spatula might, but Dennis presses the plate in closer, and she realises he wants her to lick it, like a dog, and she won't, *she won't.*

She grabs the plate, runs a finger through the orange splat, and presses the finger into her mouth. The flavour pops like sweet and sour sauce with a sparkling fizzle of an aftertaste like Champagne and the golden embers that flew up to burn her hands. It tastes perfect. It's just the consistency that's wrong. She closes her eyes and savours it, hiding in the moment.

Dennis *tsks.* "Clean that up. Get out of my sight."

"Yes, chef."

He stomps off and Ava lets herself slump.

Zach frowns after him. He has his arms crossed over his chest—to hug and comfort himself or to look bigger, it's hard to tell. "He's way harsher to you than to me."

"You have a week on me," she says, scraping her plate into the trash. The egg has developed a film over the top. "Congrats on your omelette. That's three days in a row it's held its shape."

"Just doesn't seem fair, is all."

"Life's not fair," she says. "Come on. That parsley isn't going to pluck itself."

His posture changes, his smile coming back out like the moon from behind a cloud. "That would be something: magical parsley that prepares itself."

"We'd be out of a job," she jokes.

"We wouldn't have to tell anyone."

"And if it was magic parsley, we wouldn't be allowed to work with it."

"Again," he says, "we don't tell anyone. Secret magic parsley. And it's not like we'd be touching it anyway, so it's not breaking rules."

"We'd just be hiding in the back and playing cards while it rips itself apart."

He grins. "I see no problem with that."

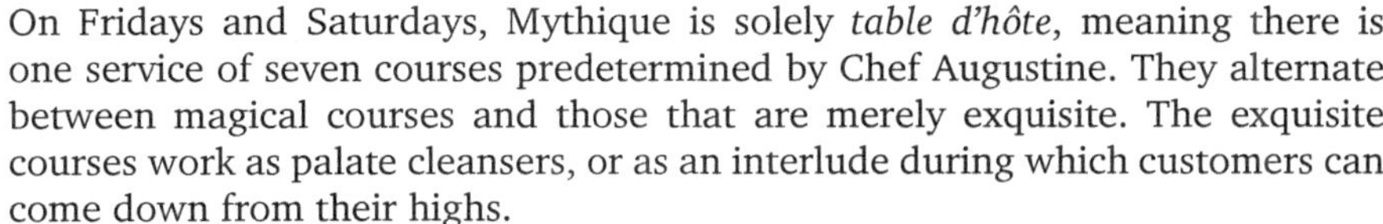

On Fridays and Saturdays, Mythique is solely *table d'hôte*, meaning there is one service of seven courses predetermined by Chef Augustine. They alternate between magical courses and those that are merely exquisite. The exquisite courses work as palate cleansers, or as an interlude during which customers can come down from their highs.

Ava has come to cherish these services since she gets to cook actual dishes eaten by real customers. It's the only time when she's treated like a full *commis* chef and not a kitchen porter. It's a chance for her to show off, to prove to herself and the other kitchen staff that she's competent. It proves it to herself mostly, because the rest of the chefs view the non-magical courses as a necessary evil, as a task well beneath their status. They're not impressed with Ava's work, but they're glad they don't have to do it, not that their relief or appreciation is voiced or enacted in any way.

Ava tries not to think about it too hard.

The rest of the kitchen loves these services because Chef Augustine will on occasion showcase one of the *Chef de Partie's* creations. A few of these have made it onto the dinner *al a carte* menu: the kraken calamari with lemon aioli, the hazelnut-crusted salmon that brings wisdom, and the salt-fried ants that bring messages from the gods. Tonight, it's the *entemetier's* big night, with the debut of his pea flourish: Avignon thrive peas marinated in the pod for weeks, soaking in the flavour of four different sauces and served as a single pea on a plate. The diner places the pea on their tongue, and it blooms in their mouth, a shoot, roots, sprouted leaves. Flavours mature one after another against the tongue as the pea grows, as it fills your mouth. It stops growing when you bite the pea, and then you chew the best salad you've ever had already in your mouth—all with unimpeachable table manners. There's something invigorating in the way you never see the pea's growth, you only track its changing form with your senses of touch and taste. There's something thrilling in the way it could choke you, and the most refined of their customers know to wait to bite the pea until the roots tickle the back of their throats in order to get the full effect, in order to catch that last little change in taste.

The junior chefs' future signature dishes are a frequent topic of discussion. Evan's had it stuck in his head that he can do four-and-twenty blackbirds baked in a pie that will burst out when you pierce the crust, and the rest of the junior chefs debate the viability of the concept at least once a day. Ava fantasises about the feathered design she'd mark into her own version of a four-and-twenty pie crust, perforating it so it would split open to look like a nest.

"My dish is going to be billdad," Zach says. He's assisting the *saucier*, whisking up a cream sauce for the first course scallops. He's back to back with Ava, who squeezes blood oranges into a strainer at the *patissier* station.

"What's that?" she asks.

"It's like if you took a turkey and a kangaroo and smooshed them together. Powerful back legs. Kind of a gamey meat, I've heard."

"You've heard? You want something you haven't tasted to be your signature dish?"

"Ah! But that's the thing: if you eat billdad, you turn into a billdad."

She twists around in disbelief. "You want to turn all the diners into kangaroo-turkeys?"

"See, I bet if I paired it with some phoenix tears in like a full-bodied red wine, it'd counteract the effect. And people would be titillated. They get to eat something dangerous. It'll be like fugu."

Ava cuts another orange in half and squeezes both sides before speaking again. "Were all billdads, at one point, people?"

He doesn't answer as he tosses the sauce in his pan, but she can feel his smirk through his back.

"That's weird." He shrugs and nods over towards the pantry, where four people in elbow-length rubber gloves are coaxing basilisk venom from fangs as long as forearms into shot glasses filled with custard. In small doses, basilisk venom gives people visions. In large quantities, it gives people seizures and paralysis.

Zach has a valid point: weird is part of the job.

"What about you? What are you going to cook for me and change my life? What's going to make Ava Mikhail famous?"

If she's honest, a pomegranate sorbet has been percolating in the back of her mind. It's been done, and pomegranate has fallen out of style lately, but there would be something lovely in its simplicity, in the lightness of the flavour. There's something magical in a well-known dish served to perfection. The bursting tang of pomegranate is one of God's gifts to Earth. The splash of red wakes her tongue, reminding her that it's a good day to be alive.

She knows better than to say this aloud.

"Golden egg in the hole," she says.

He laughs, "Oh, screw you."

"If you ladies are done gossiping," Mario, the *saucier*, shouts, "I'm thirty seconds out on these scallops."

"Thirty seconds heard," Zach sings.

Ava hands the strained blood orange juice to Christos, the Greek *patissier*, who converts them faster than she can follow into a filling, and spreads it across the freshly cut triangles of croissant dough that Ava's prepared over the past few days using the only bag of regular old flour they have, which she found hiding under a shelving unit in the pantry. As he shifts to the candied topping that will sit on the venom shot to give it a nice crunch, Ava takes his place to shape the croissants, her fingers flaring to lengthen the legs. She proofs them, brushing on a golden egg wash, which she could make, since Christos is too busy to remember she shouldn't.

At the butcher station, a small crowd has gathered as one Ibong Adarna after another is carved and transferred to the *rotisseur*. The bird is served for its healing qualities. It's said to be particularly curative for old-rich-guy disorders, but whether that's a quirk of the bird or a quirk of the people who tended to eat the bird is an easily solved mystery that no one cares to look into. It's much more fun for the junior chefs to hypothesise. Tonight, it's the fourth course, served roasted over a bed of gold leaves with lemon sauce.

"You are going to be so juicy," the *boucher* coos, holding up a plucked bird for inspection, then laying it on the block and removing its head with a chop. "Yes, you are."

A *commis* chef hums along at the newly severed head, "Look at the fat on you. Stunning. Oh, you're gonna make good broth."

"For an albatross and wild rice soup maybe. Nice and subtle," says another, touching the Ibong Adarna's head the way he'd take a child's face by the chin and bending to look into its eyes.

Ava catches the eye of the *garde* manager, Elisabetta, who is preparing the gold leaf salad on the other side of their shared counter. Ava rolls her eyes with a smile. Elisabetta stares blankly at Ava for a moment. Then sneers, "What?"

Ava realises there's no shared joke. "Nothing. Just—"

"Just you think because we both have ovaries, I'm your new BFF?"

"What? No."

"That's 'No, chef.'"

There's something blocking Ava's throat, as if she's swallowed one of the magic peas by mistake. "No, chef."

"Good. Unlike, some people I could name, I don't talk to fresh meat. Get back to work."

"Yes, chef."

Elisabetta goes back to her rapid prep, ignoring Ava completely, and Ava ducks her head back to her work. She has to be stone, she reminds herself. She isn't here to make friends. What does she care if people don't like her? She's here to do a job. She sets the pastries aside to rise just as the scallop first course goes out, a stream of wait staff gliding from the counter out into the dining room.

Ava has point for the third course: impeccable French onion soup with crusty baguette, made again with the bag of boring old flour that might be Ava's actual new BFF. She'll serve the soup with pear and apple slices simmered in brown sugar as a sweet dipping option for the bread, and sundried tomatoes with salty anchovies and capers as a savory option. Her mouth waters and her cheeks flush just thinking about it. She checks the soup before sliding over to the sauté station to start caramelising the apples and pears on two burners, simmering the anchovies on two more. Mario checks over her shoulder, gives one of the pans a flip, and nods before shifting back to his bigger project of the lemon sauce for the Ibong Adarna. When the venom shots go out, he sets his lemon sauce to simmer and takes over the anchovies, tossing in strips of sundried tomato mumbling, "Pick it up, Ava. Pick it up."

She tests a pear with a fork, finding it tender and oozing juice. She starts plating the fruit into square dip bowls. Mario appears next to her halfway through, spooning the savoury option into matching bowls. "Pick it up," he says, more urgently than before. He's finished before she is, although her pears are much neater.

"Ava! Oven!" Christos shouts, and she's slicing baguette, which is whisked away even as she slices. She turns to ladle the soup, but it's already being done, and she follows behind, placing baguette into the soup bowls and grating cheese over the top.

"Let's go, people!"

Ava's cheeks burn from the heat of the burners and the dawning realisation that she's late. Late, late, late, moving as quickly as she can even as Zach swoops in and takes the bread from her, dropping pieces into place, *bam bam bam*. The wait staff is already lined up at the pass, the plates set with two square dipping bowls each and a gaping space where the soup should go. Dennis grabs bowls out from under her, then grabs the cheese block from her hand, chops it in half and hands it back, moving down the row of soup bowls and grating along with her, faster than her. The soups are not getting enough cheese.

"Ava! Now!" Augustine. His face is as red as hers.

She gasps, "Ten seconds, chef!" and grates as quickly as she can without shredding herself, without serrating the cheese edges, without the long slivers breaking into a short mess, trying to go faster, faster, steady, faster.

"Now!"

"There!" She jumps back as the last bowl is swept out from under her and delivered to the counter for plating. Augustine, Dennis, and Elisabetta swarm the counter, wiping spilled soup from the sides of bowls, the edges of plates fast, fast, fast, steady, fast. Elisabetta gets in Dennis's way, colliding an elbow with a hip, and they explode in swears, and Chef Augustine barks at both of them and sweeps in to wipe away the mess they made. "If we'd had these bowls two minutes ago…" "…Dicking around…" "…can't hack it in a real kitchen." Dennis steps back, lifting both hands in the air as the last plate is swept onto a tray and the last of the waitstaff hurries for the dining room.

Ava presses her hands to her hot cheeks. Embarrassment tastes bitter on her tongue.

The second the door to the front of the house stops swinging, Chef Augustine rounds on her. "The hell was that?"

"I was too slow, chef."

"Damn right you were too slow. The cheese only melts if it's hot. It's not hot if you let it sit. It cools, Ava. It's useless."

"Yes, chef."

"You nearly ruined a whole course."

"I'm sorry, chef."

"Where do you think you are right now? Does this look like some leisurely lunch in a Tuscan olive orchard? Is everyone here sitting around a table, watching you cut a baguette in slow motion. Are you hallucinating right now? Does this look like an olive grove to you?"

"No, chef."

"Where are you?"

"Your kitchen, chef."

"*My* kitchen, and no one here is drinking and enjoying witty conversation while you plate like a little priss. Who's the only person here that gets to plate like a little priss?"

"You, chef."

"Me. And when the *saucier* says to pick it up, you pick it up."

As she says, "Yes, chef," Zach says, "She just wanted it to be perfect."

There isn't enough air in the room. Chef Augustine's anger focuses. He turns with painful slowness towards Zach, and says in a deadly quiet voice, "Excuse me?"

Every single chef stills, poised for fight or flight, waiting for the land mine Zach just stepped on to erupt, not daring to breathe the air that tastes so strongly of smoke. Every single chef but Zach, who is too big an idiot to read the room. "She was being careful. She's trying her best to make everything she does perfect."

Ava may be having an aneurysm, because this is surely what it feels like when a blood vessel pops in your brain.

"Was I talking to you?" Augustine says.

Zach looks befuddled, like he's genuinely confused to hear he wasn't part of this conversation, like he only just realised that Augustine is ticked.

"Let me make this real clear," Augustine says, his voice still too quiet and too measured, "since it seems no one has told you this simple, basic fact. You too," he points at Ava without looking away from Zach, "and any of you other screw-ups who may not realise how food works. If the food is not all ready at the same time, it is not perfect. One part is cold. One part is hot. The cheese doesn't melt. They don't go together. If you're taking too long, worrying about not being perfect, you're not just an idiot, but a coward. You hear that?" He swerved to face Ava again. "A coward too afraid to cook in the big leagues. A coward who lets other people fight her battles."

She opens her mouth to argue, to say she never wanted Zach to butt in. She never asked for that. She doesn't want his help. She doesn't need his help. But a sharp look from Augustine reminds her not to talk back, not to defend herself.

Her mouth snaps closed, reopening to say, "Yes, chef."

Chef Augustine shouts to the kitchen, "Four more courses! Get back to work!" And life jerks into motion again.

She ducks her head to hide her face as she pulls down the croissants to proof them a second time. Christos doesn't make eye contact. Somewhere off to the side, she can hear Elisabetta snort.

She can't defend herself, and no one can stand up for her.

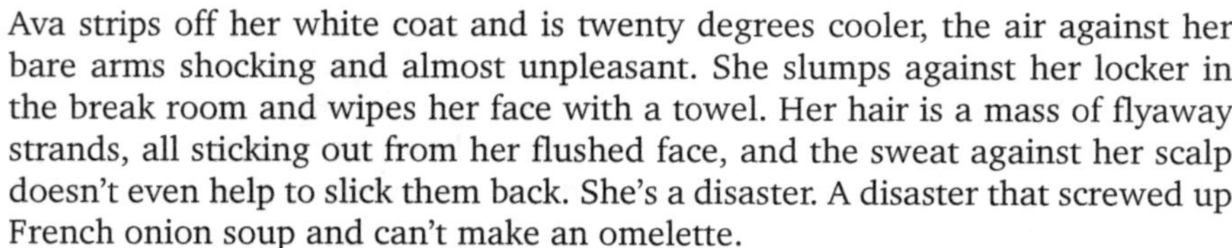

Ava strips off her white coat and is twenty degrees cooler, the air against her bare arms shocking and almost unpleasant. She slumps against her locker in the break room and wipes her face with a towel. Her hair is a mass of flyaway strands, all sticking out from her flushed face, and the sweat against her scalp doesn't even help to slick them back. She's a disaster. A disaster that screwed up French onion soup and can't make an omelette.

She's debating taking a long hot bath with a hard cider balanced on the tub rim against plopping straight into her bed without taking off her shoes. It's after midnight and her arms are sore, she's asleep on her feet, and she's so punchy she feels drunk.

So, of course, Zach picks that moment to make his entrance. He opens the locker next to her, sighing a few times more than necessary.

When she doesn't speak or even open her eyes, he takes the plunge. "If they'd been helping with the soup course instead of focusing so much on the Ibong Adrna, it would have gone fine. No one should expect you to get that full course ready by yourself. I should have stepped up and helped out sooner."

Ava's felt a whole slew of emotions in this kitchen. Embarrassment. Disappointment. Fear. Anxiety. But never before has she felt rage. It's a rage that spikes and flashes and suddenly she's yelling. "I don't need your help! I don't need anyone's help. I can plate a damn soup course. Back off."

His eyes get all sympathetic. "Don't be so hard on yourself. You did your best."

"You really think that's my best? That's my peak? That? That's who you think I am and what I can do?"

"What—"

"Screw you and your infantilising bullshit. I'm sick of it. I don't need you protecting me or standing up for me or fighting my battles. I'm a grown woman, and I'm a professional chef in a professional kitchen. Back. Off."

He stares at her, his mouth hanging limp.

"Do you not get what it looks like when you pull stunts like that?" she says.

"When *I* pull stunts?"

"Yes. You. You are at fault here."

"Chef Augustine's the one that got in your face. He and Dennis are the ones who are supposed to manage the workload."

"I messed up, Zach. That happens. I deserved to get chewed out, because I messed up. I don't deserve you treating me like a baby in front of everybody. That makes me look weak, like I'm waiting for some white knight to come rescue me. It's hard enough in there without looking any weaker than I already look."

"I don't think you look weak," he says.

She takes a breath, the tiredness crashing over her. "I'm a woman," she says. "That doesn't make me weak, but it sure as hell makes those people see me that way."

She grabs her coat and bag from her locker and stomps out, leaving him standing, speechless, slumped, and alone.

The next day, Ava drops a bag of Swedish fish into Zach's lap, and he bashfully hands her a cheese Danish that he picked up for her. They eat their peace offerings shoulder to shoulder and pretend all is forgiven.

On a Tuesday morning a week later, Ava makes a perfect golden omelette. Something clicks, and her every move is assured, controlled, her muscles relaxed and her hands deft, and she knows she has it before she plates. She's got this. She gets this. She's levelled up, and she can do anything.

Dennis tilts the plate back and forth, assessing the golden sparkles that catch in the light. For the first time in all the days she and Zach have had the fork sitting ready, Dennis reaches for it, cuts off a piece, inspects the fluffiness, the consistency, then pops the bite in his mouth and chews, eyes on the plate. He nods once. "Good," he says, and Ava punches a fist in the air.

Zach shrieks and grabs her around the waist, lifting her in the air and spinning her around, shouting, "You did it! You did it! You did it!" She can't help but laugh.

"Jesus Christ, did that noise come from you?" Elisabetta sneers. "Grow a pair."

There's a round of imitating squawks, like rowdy penguins. A few of the junior chefs do little twirls, their arms held out to their sides. To Ava, their display is entertaining in how much they don't realise they should be embarrassed, and she peeks over at Zach in hopes they can both snicker about it. Instead, she finds that Zach doesn't agree. He's rubbing the back of his ducked head, shifting uncomfortably.

As they disperse, Mario looks Zach up and down, reassessing. He pointedly turns toward Zach's burnt omelette, then back to Zach. "Huh," he says. A hum of agreement comes from the group.

Zach's ears turn red when he's emotional, something the rest of the group picked up on only a touch slower than Ava.

Her joy fades. She isn't going to let everyone ruin her moment. She isn't.

Christos, with fingers that seem too thick to do the delicate work she's seen him do, slaps a hand on her shoulder and steers her toward the pastry station. "Congrats," he says. "Now the real hell starts."

Zach makes his perfect omelette the next day. Ava rushes in for a high-five, but he shakes his head in a subtle motion and avoids eye contact. He heads off to the *rotisseur* station without any fanfare. It dawns on Ava that his victory over the omelette is null and void. He got beat by a girl.

The learning curve at the *patissier* station hits Ava like a wall. They use golden eggs in everything, and while she can now whisk them up and make an omelette in her sleep, she has to learn brand new procedures for quiche and cookie dough and cake batter. The bronze wheat flour, the amaranth flour, the almond flour, and the rye touched by a Roggenmuhme all interact with the eggs in unintuitive ways. The ritual of removing flour from its bag involves opening the bags as quietly as possible and singing specific songs or reciting specific prayers or ringing certain bells as you scoop and measure and pour into mixing bowls. The kitchen has sets of gold, onyx, and porcelain measuring cups and spoons, and memorizing which ingredient can touch which measuring spoon has Ava's head spinning. Every time she thinks she finds a pattern, an exception pops up and flour explodes into a puff of black ash into her face. The cooking times are determined by smell rather than sight or pesky digital timers, and Christos tells her the bread is almost done when it smells like burnt plastic and then suddenly turns over and smells like garlic and honey, and he has it out of the oven before it starts to smell like strawberries, which means it's ruined. The kneading of dough involves elaborate dances of protective charms done with snapping fingers and twitching crosses drawn in the air with pinkies while her hands are already filled with a rolling pin. She must roll some doughs with bottles of two-hundred-year-old honey mead, which Christos then splashes over the pastry in a way that stops Ava's heart every time.

It's such that she has to ask Christos to check her before she uses any tool at all, and it's wearing on both their patience. Christos doesn't have a *commis* chef working under him, because he keeps dismissing them, sending them to the pantry or the entremetier when he decides they can't hack it in magical pastries. The amount of time he gives his potential assistants varies from a couple months to a couple days, and Ava feels the pressure to perform building inside her with each hour she continues to be dead weight. Without additional help, Christos covers the *patissier* station mostly alone, and with the added burden of teaching her, their situation lumbers along at an ever more frantic pace.

"You're a pastry chef," Christos tells her, in what comes so close to a pep talk that she almost cries with gratitude. "It's hard."

The only thing that saves her is that pastry involves so much prep work that she's not constantly rushing to make dishes as orders come in during service and screwing up in real time like everyone else. Like Zach. Her schedule changes so she comes in before the protesters gather, before the sun breaks through the front windows, and she and Christos bake bread and croissants and rolls and crusts and English muffins and cupcakes and ice cream and icing and fondant and chocolate sauce and candies and truffles and spun-sugar accent pieces. They prep, and when an order comes in during service, all she has to do is pause what she's prepping (because even during services she's constantly prepping for the next day, for the day after), slice a piece of cake or fry up some dough real fast, throw hot fudge over it, send it out, wash her hands, and go back to her prep work. The bread they make is handed over to the pantry so other chefs can use it for sandwiches at lunch service and they never have to look at it again.

It's Friday lunch and Ava's working on the leviathan milk cake, the seventh course of that night's *table d'hôte*. Christos made the cake, a serpentine log like a cinnamon roll of white cake that melts in your mouth, swirled with blue leviathan milk that makes those who eat it fearless for about twelve hours. He's left the decorating to her, as it's easily inside her current skill set and he has phyllo dough to make because she botched her last attempt. She pulls out fondant that she made earlier, covers the cake, which is about three feet long and takes up a big swath of their counter space, trims, and on another sheet of fondant airbrushes colour and machines out scale shapes with a cookie cutter that Christos made himself. Place the scales overlapping on the cake, never losing her rhythm, *chick chick chick chick*, another sheet of fondant, airbrush colour, cut out scales, place, repeat. When the repetitive motion starts to cramp her hands, she pulls out the world's tiniest paintbrush and paints shadows on the scales. She gives herself three minutes to do that, before she forces herself back, another sheet of fondant, *chick chick chick chick*.

"How far out on the ants?"

"Two out on ants."

"Two soup *du jours* on deck."

"One vanilla ice cream, one brownie."

"One vanilla ice cream, one brownie heard," Ava calls. Christos is still working the phyllo dough and doesn't lose his rhythm. She sets down her airbrush and grabs a devil's brownie from its tray on a cooling shelf. The servers tell the customers when the brownies come fresh out of the oven, so they never last long. She moves to the freezer, scoops vanilla prickly pear ice cream. Chocolate sauce, vanilla bean decoration, and they're ready to go. "Ice cream and brownie up." She washes her hands and gets back to her leviathan.

"Man, Ava," one of the *commis* from the roast station calls, "it must be nice to not have a real job."

Half the kitchen hoots. Ava ignores them. *Chick chick chick chick.*

The offender is slicing roast sun cow slices for a sandwich, which will use bread Ava more or less successfully made this morning, more or less on her own.

"Naw, dude, it looks good," another guy says. "Ignore them, Ava. Hey! You know how I've got this Dodge B-series van. You think you could paint a mural on the side of it for me?"

More hoots, and the guys pick that one up and carry it.

"Like a T-rex fighting a wizard."

"And some spiralling galaxies in the background."

"And a sexy minotaur."

"Whoa! Whaaat?"

"What? Minotaur ladies can be sexy!"

They fall upon each other and thankfully move on from Ava.

The guys all act like beautiful plating is superfluous to the manly art of butchering magical animal meats and getting stoned on deadly venoms, like their delicate, pink bites of veal on beds of finely sliced poached pears are the manliest things ever to be invented. They act like the customers couldn't get leviathan milk off the street for $20 a hit, and they ignore that the customers come here and spend $30 on dessert instead. They come for the safety and cultural endorsement in which consuming it is wrapped, for the elitism of not having to call it a "hit."

"Hey, Ava," one of the guys calls, unfortunately bringing things back around to her. "Since you're not doing anything, could you find me a left-handed spatula?"

She flips him off over her shoulder.

"Hey, hey. What do you call a cake decorator without parents?"

"Homeless."

Ava's rhythm stutters. That punchline was provided by none other than Zach.

She's cold inside the oven of her white jacket, disloyalty jolting her system.

Christos appears at her elbow with impeccable timing, pressing a cold bowl of baklava filling covered in saran wrap into her hands. "Fill these." He takes over the leviathan scales.

No one mocks Christos for his profession.

As she spreads baklava filling over phyllo dough, she peeks over her shoulder to where Zach jumps back from a flare from a burner, barely keeping hold of the pan in his hand. The *rotisseur* calls him a sissy and snatches it from him, pulling the salmon from the pan. Zach has already moved on to rotate a unicorn leg on a spit, and without something immediate that needs doing, he looks up to catch Ava watching him in disapproval. Ava curses herself. She wishes he hadn't seen her.

He checks that the *rotisseur* is busy but not too busy and sneaks over. She wishes he wouldn't.

"Hey," he says.

"Go back to work," she says, spreading crushed nuts and Manuka honey. They're both going to get in trouble when Mario notices him away from his station: him for wandering off, her for distracting him or luring him away or something.

He takes a breath, maybe to apologise, but the way she's ignoring him keeps him quiet.

Instead, he says, "You need to lay it on thicker than that," and takes the filling from her hands, spreading a thicker layer. He grins at her, like this is a peace offering.

She stares at him, unable to control what her face is doing. This is her station. She's the assistant pastry chef. She knows what she's doing, and while, yeah, in a typical baklava you'd want it thicker to get the flavour, here the strong honey will overwhelm it and the phyllo dough won't cook. Where the hell does he get off telling her how to do her job? They're the same freaking level.

Christos makes a noise that will require he wash his hands afterward. "Get away from my baklava, idiot." He scrapes off the layer of filling.

Zach doesn't care. He slaps her shoulder and heads back to the unicorn, where he snatches a brush and a jar of marinade from another assistant who wasn't laying it on thick enough and does it himself.

"Idiots," Christos repeats. "Marinating in their own stupidity."

Ava ties on her apron one morning and realises that two months have passed and she's still at the pastry station. She scoops amaranth flour with the porcelain measuring cup without checking and hums the bronze wheat's favourite song without worrying herself into a sweat over it. She stirs the dough for rye bread clockwise and devil's brownies batter in a seven-pointed star. Christos mentions that he likes her sourdough better than his own, and then tells her to stop smiling.

It's hard to tell how Zach is faring. Like everyone, he shivers when he comes into the break room and takes off his coat, air conditioned as it is and dressed as they all are for the heat of the kitchen, which only increases when they put on their white coats at service. They are as scantily clad as they can get away with without violating health codes. Zach has a full-body shudder every single morning that he covers with over-exaggeration: bouncing on his toes and flapping his arms and motor-boating his lips. He covers discomfort with jokes and enthusiasm.

It carries into the kitchen with his constant talk about the billdad, which has only grown worse when Chef Augustine caught wind of it and interrogated him about every nitty-gritty aspect of his vision. Should they smoke the meat? Should they marinate it in the antidote or have it be the customer's responsibility to drink with every bite? Then he announced that they would do a test run of the antidote wine.

Then he announced that they would cook a billdad.

Not for the Friday night dinner, but for themselves. A proof of concept. None of them have tried it before, and he doesn't care how hot an idea it is, if it ends up tasting like budget deer meat, he isn't serving it.

Zach and Ava and everyone peer over Chef Augustine's shoulders as he cuts open the Styrofoam cooler from the truck and lifts the lid. The billdad hasn't been plucked, but its plumage has been folded and crammed into the cooler. It's surrounded by bags of dry ice and its oversized back legs rear up well over its back, folded in on itself to fit. Zach *tsks* and reaches in to gently unpack it. After some careful extensions of its neck, some checks of the meat and malleability, the beast is stretched out on the counter like a Thanksgiving turkey with a neck too long and legs too big. Its plumage is dull and drab, brown with only a hint of red. Zach and Augustine run their hands over it again and again, smoothing feathers, rearranging. "Nothing to be done for the plumage," Zach says.

Some turkeys have layers on layers of beautiful, iridescent plumage, which you wouldn't know from construction paper hand-turkeys made in elementary school or the images of the emancipated and the force-fed turkeys that come out of turkey farms. Free-range birds are glorious and terrifying, and pictures Ava has seen of billdads in the wild attest to this.

Chef Augustine agrees, "We'll need a better supplier," and then slaps Zach on the back and leaves him to the plucking.

Ava leaves him to it as well. With him working on that, she and the other junior chefs have to take on some of his prep work, and she doesn't want to think about billdad suppliers. She imagines billdad farms that bred them in their billdad form, which she's not sure is possible. She imagines sinister men offering "turkey burgers" to homeless people, to kids in group homes, to guys in jail, to people in retirement homes. She thinks about who this billdad used to be, how they came to be this way, if they chose it or if it was chosen for them, if their family knows what happened to them.

She thinks of the protesters outside and their reaction to the creature lying on the counter. Would there be more protestors if they knew about the billdad? Would there be television coverage and petitions? Would they shift from chanting and holding signs to throwing stones through the front window? Would they swarm into the kitchen, trampling the chefs under their feet, lifting the billdad over their heads to carry it away? Would the kitchen change afterward to a kinder, gentler place?

No. People might care, but they would care in a way where they *tsk* and shake their heads. Nothing would change.

She shivers and starts making bread, bread made with bronze wheat that when it rests on your tongue, you—and only you—can hear angels singing. Ava's always heard it more like a damp finger circling the rim of a wine glass, but maybe that's what angels sound like, and maybe everyone hears something slightly different and the experience is not only life-changing but personal.

She thinks about how all her favourite magical foods are vegetarian. Bronze wheat. Honeysuckle nectar. Fire honey. Pomegranates.

Zach finishes plucking the billdad after the action in the kitchen has reached cruising altitude. Another group clumps around him as he turns to butchering. He has the idea to just cook the legs. They're the meatiest part and the real draw of the creature, since the wings are small and the breast uninspiring. But there's a push to use every piece of it, and although Ava knows deep down it's fuelled by respect for the life given so they could have this meat, the push is voiced in terms of occupational integrity and pragmatism. "It's expensive. You're not throwing out half the bird." "Use the breast in billdad Kiev?" "Use the giblets in a gravy?" "At least freeze the head and neck for broth." "One whole bird could work for a tasting menu. Everyone should only eat one bite anyway. Don't trust people to eat a whole leg. They'll get complacent halfway through." "So what? Some people get dark meat and some get light?" "Sure. Individualised!" "Consistency!"

With the bird carved, Zach turns to the antidote wine. He mixes up a glass, a concoction of Merlot, phoenix tears, cloves, cardamom, cinnamon, and orange zest, but he stirs "like a lady making a daiquiri," and the roast master takes over with his unsung mixology skills. He practically struts as he mixes, puffing out his chest like he's flexing his muscles on a beach rather than peacocking for his co-workers. They pull a dragon crest sauce from the fridge and pull back the plastic wrap. Zach eats a spoonful and then chokes down a swig of wine through his coughing that he tries to keep locked in his mouth, but the coughs slip out in billowing clouds of smoke and spluttered wine. After the first sip, he starts chugging it as if it will quench his fiery belches, and five people shout at him to cut it out. He sets down the glass, twists his face like he's sucked a lemon, and shudders. He opens his mouth to another round of fireworks, and the mixing duties are taken from the roast master and given over to Dennis, who's unusually friendly today. They're like sharks in the water, gleeful for spectacle and violence. They claim to be there to help Zach succeed, but it feels like they're there to watch him fail, ready to kick him to the curb if he turns into a bird or catch him and embrace him for days and days of more trials.

Dennis's batch dulls the flames from Zach's mouth, and one whole side of the kitchen applauds. There are much less explosive magical ingredients they could have used for a test.

Maybe it's her own tension she feels, but Christos seems to get more and more agitated as the day goes on. They do their work in silence, barely looking up at the showboating distraction on the other side of the kitchen, barely speaking to anyone as no one bothers to speak to them. They carry on their prep until she catches Christos watching her.

When she pauses, he nods and goes back to his candied blood oranges. "Someday I'm going to open a bakery."

He says it so quietly that at first she's not sure she heard him right. Then the group behind them explodes again. The billdad is on the grill.

No one seems to be working—all watching Zach watch the bird. There was excitement and distraction when the entremetier first tried his peas, an excitement that kept going each time they were brought back out for a new test, but that was nothing. It's like they're all eager to watch Zach put his life in danger, ready to watch him become a kangaroo before their eyes.

Ava whips up meringue, taking her frustration out on the poor egg mixture, which collapses, reverting back into golden egg goop. Thankfully no one is watching but Christos, who says nothing and takes the bowl from her after she's cleaned up her mess. He hands her a saucepan of heated caramel for the decorative cages he's been making and does the meringue himself. The acceptance of emotion is not lost on her, and she sets to drizzling the caramel with exceptional care.

When the billdad is ready, Ava's work stops as if a force has halted her hands for her. She's frozen, watching the plating. She lifts her eyes to watch Zach's face, the way the sweat has run from his temples, the glitter of his eyes like he's got the best quip ready to go and it's going to make her spit her drink across the table at family meal, the way his T-shirt rides up his human arms. She can't watch. She can't look away. Everyone is frozen or chanting, "Zach! Zach! Zach! Zach!"

She lowers her saucepan. She can't watch this. She has to leave. She has to throw up.

Christos grabs both her arms, holds her there. Her heart is beating too hard to tell if the hold is restraining or grounding. "You want to be a chef?" he says, right next to her ear. "Then you stay, and you watch." He shakes her, and she sucks in a breath for the first time in minutes. "Watch."

The billdad is arranged, and the plate's turned a quarter turn for effect.

"This is what you're in for. This is what it's like. It's not going to get better," Christos continues.

Chef Augustine nods at Zach.

"You can break now, but then you're through."

And he's right. This is what it's like, what it will be like. If she can't bear it another second, if she can't fathom a life of this, day after day after day until she dies or quits or pushes her way through to some safe and friendly place more mythical than the food they serve, then she can walk away. And if she walks away, she'll give up on a dream.

She has to be stone.

Zach picks up a fork and knife. Grinning, he cuts off a bite, checks the colour, wipes it through the sauce, and pops it in his mouth.

Ava becomes stone. Zach becomes a monster.

Memories

Featured in Issue #74

...Frank Hebben
(translated by Richard Kunzmann)

*A voice from an old film is heard, muted mono sound, accompanied
by two beat music. Raindrops tap lightly against the window.*

"I'll buy it," said the girl with the butterfly eyes. "How many fragments is it?"

The broker bent over the transmitter, a gadget like a cube, wires left and right ending with golden connections for the forehead.

"Fifteen."

"What, fifteen?" The girl pried her connection off with two fingers. "That's more than three memories."

"Of the best quality," the broker added and put on his best salesman's smile. "Crystal clear images, pure emotions. We only take alpha memories."

"Expensive."

"For good reason." The broker opened his hands. "This one dates back to 1964, Western Europe, France perhaps; it's more than two hundred years old." His smile broadened. "La Bohéme, if you know what I mean."

"La Bohéme," the girl repeated thoughtfully. "All right, fine. Do you take bad ones too?"

"It depends."

"I have an experience from factory school, two nights in prison, and the murder of my mother."

The broker drew air in through his teeth. "Murder? This is a reputable business, little lady. You can't exchange that here. Memories of books or films our government had destroyed—those we'll gladly take. Sunsets, memories of animals and plants, a picnic in the woods; have you got fragments along those lines?"

"No," the girl answered sadly. Her eyes glistened with a thousand colours. "Oh wait, I once had a dog."

"A dog? There are collectors for that sort of thing. Which breed?"

"I don't know. It had royal blue fur."

The broker held up a hand. "No artificials, sorry."

"I'll have to think about it a bit more," whispered the girl. She pulled the hood of her plastic coat over her head and pulled the strings tight. "Later."

"Come by again the moment something good has happened to you." The broker took off his own connection. "I bid you a good evening."

Acrid rain falls drop by drop like blood, painted red by neon light. I'm approaching a club in the shadows

Inside voices were artificially muted; only a pleasant murmur escaped the booths along the walls. The girl had seated herself at a window overlooking the street, and watched endless waves of people pushing by.

"What can I get you?" asked a waitress. She put aside a tray laden with cups, pulled out a pen and writing pad. She waited attentively.

"Sunburn without ice." The girl did not look at her. "A double."

"Lousy day?"

"Lousy life."

The rain fell. Two men went by, a woman, a man, a police officer. The girl turned away quickly.

"What's your name?" asked the waitress.

"Céline."

"Chin up, Céline, don't let it get you down."

"Sunburn without ice, double."

"Coming up."

Céline stripped off her sling bag and plastic coat, hung them up on a hook. When the waitress came back with her drink she immediately paid the exact amount, without a tip, and burrowed deep into the corner created by the window and upholstery. Her breath bloomed against the window. She carefully raised the glass to her lips and took a nip. Closing her eyes, Céline thought of her favourite memory, the only good one she still had; all the others had been sold.

The sea is vast and blue, so cold and clear. It's even breathing in and out. The sun glares above and birds draw their circles in the sky.

The cocktail did the trick: there was a warm tingling in her stomach, like love, and Céline sighed with relish. Things were much better now. She ordered another glass.

"Sunburn?" asked the waitress.

"Double."

"Coming up."

"Wait," said Céline. "I'm looking for someone who's into bad memories."

"Want to get rid of one, don't you, dear? What is it—an unhappy love?

Honey, we're all bothered by them."

"Do you know of someone?" Céline asked softly.

"Maybe The Needle will take it off you. Bad memories and new drugs, they keep her going, even if she can't feel anything anymore. Try it; offer it to her. She hangs around near the harbour, at the market of dreams."

"I know where it is."

"Look for her behind the stands. I'll bring you that cocktail."

"Thanks."

When the waitress returned to her table, Céline downed the drink, paid and got up. She put on her coat, grabbed her bag and left the bar. At the next corner she took a left and followed the streets until she reached the market at the harbour. It did not take her long to find The Needle leaning tiredly against a streetlight, a woman in her twilight years with an emaciated body, cheekbones pushing out of a gaunt face.

"They call you The Needle?"

"Who wants to know?" The woman's bright crystal blue eyes bored into her; neon implants.

"Bad memories, do you take them?" asked Céline.

"You lose your teddy bear?" The Needle's lips pulled back in what might have been a smile.

"I'm talking about my mother's murder."

There was a brief silence.

"You stupid thing," said The Needle. "Still wet behind the ears and you've already ruined your life."

"No, no, it wasn't me."

"Oh. Is it good quality?"

"I think so."

"Okay," said The Needle. "Let me see." She reached for her belongings propped up against the streetlight, fished out a cube, and attached one end to her forehead. "Come here, I'll take a look." The Needle waved her closer.

Céline reached for the weapon concealed in her bag, hesitated, then stepped closer. "I want something nice for it."

"Nice? Like a memory of snow?"

"You have something like that?" Céline asked astonished.

"Me?" Laughter shook The Needle. "Sure, kiddo!"

"What do you have, then?"

"How about something with clowns? An old dream with clowns."

"Alright. Why not?"

"Come closer."

Dark night has fallen in the alley. A scalpel is drawn, no, two, engraved blades, a dragon on one, the devil on the other. One arcs out, the other does too. Blood is spilled everywhere.

"Now it's my turn," said The Needle. She pressed a second transmitter button.

I see clowns in bright colours, laughing. Pies fly, tricycles spill
"Tatoo-tata! Tatoo-tata! Look! Here comes a fire engine!"

Céline giggled cheerfully. She did not know why, but she felt relieved. A shadow over her soul had lifted. Relaxed, she took off the connection.

"A great trade," she said to The Needle.

"You liked it? I'm happy, too: strong emotions, fear." She thought back to that night. "Yes, it's a good one," she said. Then, "Wait a minute, I know this guy!"

"Who?"

"The one with the scalpels."

"I don't know what you're talking about." Céline turned to leave.

"I'm talking about the killer who's got your mother on his conscience."

She stopped dead in her tracks. "What?" The sunburn's effect on her evaporated. "Salvador Dali."

"Dali?" Céline asked as she turned around. At the same time she began unzipping her bag.

"That's his street name." The Needle reached into her coat and dug around for a tin, opened it and took out three pills, which she put into her mouth. Her neon pupils flickered, first becoming yellow then blood red. "He's been hunting around in the golden quarter, collecting organs and skin for his creations. There are buyers for that kind of… art. I saw an exhibition, just recently."

"I want all those memories."

"Little girl, leave it alone. He's dangerous."

"I want them all." Céline pulled out a gun. "All of them! And I want mine back, too!"

The vast blue sea reflects light into hall. I see paintings on the walls,
cold and clear. Fat and organs are exposed. He's even breathing.
He laughs and smiles. I see greedy delight in his face as a woman shows
interest and then buys them for DeLanys. The sun still glares above and the
birds still draw their circles.

"No!" screamed Céline as she tore the connection from her forehead. "You've ruined it with this piece of junk!" She pressed the tip of her gun against The Needle's throat.

"I—" She choked. "What did I—"

Céline flicked the gun's safety off. "Not that one, anything but that one!"

"I'm sorry, I didn't want to—" The Needle slowly sank to her knees. "Please."

"You shit!" roared Céline.

She pulled the pistol back. Two tears escaped her eyes. "It was all I had!"

Crying, she turned and bolted.

I see houses, streets and people, no more than shadows behind glass.
I feel hope, sorrow and pain. There is no way out of this labyrinth.

The young, steel-blond saleswoman at DeLanys wore a white doctor's coat; why was not immediately apparent to the average buyer. Céline pushed open the glass door leading into the studio and stepped up to the first exhibited painting: The Mage on Cardboard, 2134.

"A wonderful portrait," said the saleswoman behind her. "The face is so expressive, even if it appears empty. Those burning eyes, the skeletal cheeks, hollow but prominent."

"How much does it cost?" Céline asked.

The woman gave a false laugh. 'Oh, you can't afford it, dear. At an auction it could easily fetch 28,000."

"Fragments?"

"Oh, please!" The saleswoman laughed. "Cash." She pointed at a rack of 3D postcards. "But we sell first-class prints, which you can send to your little friends."

Céline turned away. "I don't like it that much." She glanced at a surgery-green curtain that divided this room from the next. "I'm more into organic art."

"Aah!" The saleswoman let her false smile spread; Céline wondered how much that must have cost her. "You've heard of it?"

"Of Dali's paintings?"

"Yes, exactly."

"I was a guest at the last exhibition."

"And you want to see them again?" the saleswoman asked. "I understand that. He is a true artist, gives you goose bumps."

"You couldn't have said it better," Céline agreed. She tried to copy the woman's smile. "Could I have a look at them now?"

"I'm alone today, and I don't really have the time for pleasantries."

"Please."

The young woman in the coat regarded Céline a long moment, then her bogus smile grew more suggestive. She winked and said, "Okay. For you, I'll make an exception, but only for a quick look."

"Thank you very much," said Céline.

"No need, come on."

She parted the curtain and let Céline pass. They walked along a long corridor, then down two flights of stairs. Through a doorway, they finally reached another studio, lit up in arctic fluorescence. Along the walls were glass cases, each one covered with a drape. Céline was led to the largest of the exhibits.

"We don't have any prints of this one." The saleswoman laughed. "So remember it well." She yanked its drape aside.

One more bad memory, thought Céline, before the shock overwhelmed her. All that stayed in her head was a rushing sound, like a television without a picture. She stood staring at what was in the case, unable to say anything.

"—naturally it's vacuum sealed to preserve it, otherwise—"

Cold sweat on her forehead.

"—death as art, that's one of the main themes of his—"

Hands shaking.

"—in his earlier period, about seven years ago—" The saleswoman broke off. "Aren't you feeling well?"

Céline dragged her eyes away from the work and looked up at the saleswoman. "What?"

"I said, are you not feeling well?"

"Oh—no, no, I'm fine; it's just really cold in here."

The woman re-covered the case with the drape. "We have to cool this room, to preserve the works." She headed for the door; Céline followed her. "That's it for now, I have to get back. Maybe we'll do this again tomorrow."

"Thanks," Céline mumbled as she tried to shake off her dizziness. "I would love to have an autograph."

"Mine?" The woman winked. "You mean his. We don't do autographs. You'd have to ask him yourself."

"When is the next exhibit? Today?"

"You mean the preview? No, what gave you that idea?"

"Where can I find Salvador Dali?"

"Darling, you're really taken with him, aren't you?" The saleswoman laughed. "It's not often that someone your age feels so strongly about modern art."

They went up the first flight of stairs. On the landing of the second, Céline stopped abruptly. "Where do I find the artist? Where?"

The woman turned around with a puzzled expression on her face. "We never give out names and addresses. Next week you'll have the opportunity—"

Céline pulled the gun from her bag and pointed it first at the woman's chest, then at her throat. "I want this shits address, now! I'm not asking a second time."

"Are you crazy?" The woman was surprisingly calm. "Put that thing away and get lost, before I call the police." She turned back to the stairs and took a few steps when Céline abruptly kicked her legs out from underneath her. The saleswoman's chin hit the edge of a step with a loud crack, and she screamed in pain.

"Where do I find the pig?" cried Céline. "Tell me!"

"He's a doctor at St. Johns Hospital." The woman was frantically touching the bridge of her nose to see if it had perhaps been broken; blood trickled from a cut on her chin. "He lives and works there."

"His name?"

"Dr Randal, his name's Randal." Groggily, the woman got to her feet. "You certainly are fanatical. Leave him alone."

"Back down." Céline brandished the pistol at her. "Move!"

She forced the woman back down the stairs and they re-entered the room with Dali's artwork.

"Against the wall."

"No, please don't," whimpered the saleswoman.

"Against the wall, I said! Your back towards me!" Céline quickly reached into her bag and took out a cube. "Now, I want every memory of me and the last fifteen minutes. Got that?"

"Yes," the woman said meekly.

Céline activated the button.

> *A girl with a bag and coat sneaks past, so much sadness in her butterfly eyes. She's alone in the world, like so many others.*

"Who are you?" the saleswoman asked, puzzled.

"I have a gun pointed at you. If you turn around, you're dead."

"You're stealing the paintings!"

"You can keep this crap!" Céline made for the exit. "I'm going to close the door now, and you're going to count to a hundred. After that you can call the cops. Stay against the wall. I don't want to shoot you."

"Yes, okay."

Céline closed the door behind her. Then she ran, up the stairs, through the gallery, out the door and into the rain, down the left, turning right, ever onward, in the direction of the golden quarter.

> *Empty faces stare at me, shiny like glass. The neon light paints bright masks of shamans, angels and demons.*

In the rain the hospital looked like a church: a broad architecture, above which shone a giant cross. Determined, Céline entered the lobby and headed straight for the reception desk.

"I'm looking for Dr Randal." She said to the duty nurse.

"What is it about?"

"He's my father. I have to speak with him. My mother died."

"Oh, you poor thing!" The nurse grabbed a list and ran a long nail down the printed lines. "Dr Randal's shift just ended. If you hurry, you might be able to catch him at the personnel entrance. Out the door, turn left, and left again at the corner."

Céline hurried back the way she came, out the revolving door and into the pouring rain. She ran past billboards and ducked into an alley in time to see a man leave the hospital side door. She stopped. "Dr Randal?"

"Yes?" He drew up and blinked against the rain.

"I've seen your paintings, your works of flesh."

Sensing something was wrong, he took a step back. "And, do you like them?"

"No," Céline replied and pulled out her pistol. "They disgust me."

"It's like that for a lot of people." Randal took another step backward and another, angling across the narrow alley. He threw a quick glance towards a minibus parked on the opposite curb. "You don't understand their message. The sweeping beauty of mankind, that's what I want to show. Nothing more, nothing less."

"And for that you're killing people? That's sick!" Céline reduced the distance between them. "Stop where you are."

"Killing? No, those already dead are my source material."

"Don't lie to me!" Céline yelled as she kept advancing. "You prey at night, in search of fresh victims like an animal. I've seen you, you piece of shit!"

Randal tried a more disarming expression. "Nonsense, you're mistaking me for someone else."

"Engraved blades, a dragon and a devil."

"Damn!" Surprisingly agile, Randal ducked towards the minibus, and tore the door open.

"Stop!"

Two gunshots rang out in the alley. One shattered the vehicle's windshield; the second tore into Randal's leg.

With an effort, the doctor heaved himself into the driver's seat. "What is it you want?"

As she approached, Céline shot him in the arm. Randal howled in pain. Unable to stop himself from slipping, he fell out the car and into the gutter.

"What do I want?" she shouted, hoarsely. "A life, a place of my own, family, friends. And to forget all of this. Say goodbye to this world, you psychopath!"

> *Blood stains his chest, like from a fist that has landed*
> *a devastating blow. His eyes are empty and white like plastic.*
> *He draws one last breath and then he's gone*

"Sister, is there anything else you want to be rid of?" the priest asked gently. "I take them all: the sad, the bad, the terrible." He lifted his hands to the heavens. "For you, I am the Lord's vessel."

"No thanks," Céline smiled and pulled her hood over her head. "I have nothing else to confess."

Day and Night Girl

Featured in Issue #76

...Rachel Chimits

If a man touches your hair, you must marry him. Even if his arm only brushes a strand and neither of you notice until it's too late, even if you're only a child, and even if he's already married. The only way marriage may be avoided in this case is if the man is a close relative, if he is someone against whom your family has a blood oath, or if you're a shaman.

Like their names, a shaman's hair may never signal another's ownership. If you come across a person who shares their name and leaves their hair unbound, then you have either found a shaman or an evil spirit.

Only a woman who has been raped cuts her hair.

I look like no one in my family, least of all my mother; but she says I am no wind-spirit child. She bore me on the steppe after two years of being with no one other than my sisters, Father, and six hundred sheep. Unless I'm the bastard get of a ram, I belong to my family. That we all know, for better or worse.

No one will ever see my hair, if I have any say in the matter. I hate it the same way I hate my two-toned skin. My body's like an autumn sky on a day of uncertain weather. The first white patches appeared at the base of both my thumbs, and I pull my sleeves over them until the patches grow and my aunty grabs my wrist.

"Oh, Voice of Wind," she says, then screams for Mother.

My cousins put on leather gloves and drag me out of the yurt. My oldest cousin wants to lock me in a goat pen—like the goat's maggoty penis that he is—but my younger cousin points out that I'll freeze.

"Sorry, Khulan," he says softly. "You have to stay here until we know if you're infectious."

"Am I sick?" I start to cry as he nods. "With what? I feel okay. What am I sick with?"

Older cousin pulls his younger brother away. "We don't know."

"Yes, you do." I hit him with a fist half the size of his. It can't hurt him, but he flinches. "Tell me!"

"Just wait here until your mother and father come."

"I'll find a way out, and you can't stop me." He knows I'll do it too. I'm not named after a wild ass for nothing.

"Don't do that. Promise me, Khulan. Aunty thinks maybe leprosy. You could get other people sick."

Then I begin to cry in earnest. My parents find me with my eyes swollen nearly shut. My father has me turn my hands every direction under a lamp. My mother pokes the white spots with needles, and I shriek at her with some pain and more rage. They look at one another, and my father shrugs. My hands are wrapped and examined daily; the white slowly spreads like frost on blades of grass, but the flesh beneath is alive.

It takes two years and a disaster to shift my skin out of the centre of family gossip. This is what happens when your aunties and mother have no weddings to plan or particularly stupid relatives to be entertaining.

The air fills with smoke that the wind can't clear, and my family watches the horizon for fire. Instead, a distant cousin of my mother's comes riding on a horse so exhausted it can't even work up a lather. I take it to a pen, its head practically hanging between its knees, give it water and hay, then run to our yurt.

Third cousin sits by the fire with a cup of salted buffalo milk tea trembling between his fingers. "The Akagi unleashed the Boars of Tadashi on the eastern steppe, and they've brought fire with them. The Northern Plains men tried to shoot them down, but now they are ash and the boars still run free."

"Have the Akagi's brains turned to mush?" Father cries. "How will they recapture the boars?"

Oldest cousin is practically hopping like a hungry flea, ready to suck up this glorious bit of history in the making. "It took Tadashi Daito forty days and nights to subdue them all—he was the greatest shaman of the age—then the Akagi warlords begged for peace and were never heard from again."

"Tadashi Daito is dead," Father says. "Unfortunately, his boars are not."

Our visitor shakes his head. "I don't think the Akagi mean to do anything. Maybe they think their island can shake the dust off their boots. The boars are our problem now."

"Maybe the High Plains Riders and their shaman will be able to do something," Mother says bitterly.

A smoky silence hangs over us all. The High Plains shaman's great grand-uncle had a blood oath with my great, great grand-cousin twice removed, but they both died of fire-throat fever before they could draw bows against one another. The blood oath isn't strictly my family's to fulfil—no one is quite sure whose it is since great, great grand-cousin had no children and alienated his relatives by being a shit-splattered ball sack—but his blood oath still puts a bad taste in everyone's mouths, like ash in our drinking water.

"There's more," third cousin says. "Tadashi's red boar has been seen running in the fire. They're calling it Tsus."

Father hisses to clear the air of that name, but suddenly I see the boar in the flames between us all like an omen, with blood splattered across his snout and wickedly curving tusks, dripping with the gore for which it has been named. They say his eyes are black as night, but that's a lie. The night is alive with a brilliant freckling of stars, and his eyes are empty and pitiless like the bled-out depths of a lamb's cut throat.

I throw my hands over my face and scream.

Tadashi Daito stared into nightmare eyes and never flinched. He waded those dead depths for forty days and nights like a man who has never known warmth or love. Even my donkey-stubborn heart can't understand how.

Mother slaps me for making a fuss, and I can't even be angry because pain makes the vision vanish. I crawl into my bed beside my sisters, and they whisper about the smoke and the fires while we unwrap our hair. Then they go silent, and my oldest sister reaches out to brush the top of my head.

"Khulan, you have white hair. Right on top of your crown."

She holds her copper mirror for me to see. Sure enough, there is a streak like hawk shit down the left side of my uneven part.

"What if it happens to our hair too?" my younger sister whines, and oldest sister hushes her, but she still makes me rewrap my hair like I have lice.

The next day we pack up the yurts, even though it isn't even close to autumn yet. My sisters and father drive the sheep while my older cousin and I oversee our small herd of goats. Holding my whip stick, I study my fingers which are almost entirely white as if I'd plunked my hands in milk.

"Hey, that nanny's running off! Heads up, brat."

I swat the offending goat then return oldest cousin's scowl. "I saw Tsus in the fire last night."

His sunburnt skin goes ashy. "Don't say his name. Don't call him."

"That's not his true name. That's just some dumb thing people called him because they're scared."

"Oh, and you're not frightened?" His boxy jaw works. "Names are never stupid. I saw him in the fire too, Khulan. His eyes could have eaten our souls, just like his name. Between you and our stupid distant cousin—you two will call him down on us."

I look at my hands again.

If my goat-penis cousin saw Tsus too, then I suppose I'm not special.

I remember my ruined hair with its horrible white streak like a comet. The death of stars always foretells inauspicious times, and I wonder if my head counts. But while the Voice of Wind might shoot down stars with his night bow, I doubt he'd bother with my hair.

Quickly, I catch a tear before oldest cousin sees it. My skin and hair have nothing to do with these troubles, no more than the burning grass or the chunks of skin caught on Tsus's tusks.

Our family flees from spot to spot for the next two years, following the light-footed antelope away from the flying ash. The white spreads across my hands and lower arms then unfolds across my chin. The boys of other families who had joined our train glance at me when they think I won't notice. I secretly look in oldest sister's copper mirror before she marries and takes it away in her trousseau. The colour has leaked up around my chin and mouth in the shape of a cicada's abandoned chrysalis. I unwrap my head and bend it to see the clay-coloured streaks in my hair. I'm as tall as oldest sister, but no one will touch my skin or my hair.

"I am safe," I whisper as I tuck my braids beneath my scarf, pull it as far up over my chin as I dare, and tug my sleeves so they cover all the way to my knuckles. "I am safe, now and forever."

Goat-penis still sees Tsus in the campfires. He goes pale and shakes, and after all the basket lights are smothered and Mother begins to snore, I hear him weeping.

He glances at me while we milk the nannies, a hopeful, desperate light in his eyes. His looks give me a sick, squirmy feeling. I want to slap him, but he's the only one who spends much time with me anymore, so I don't. I also don't tell him I haven't seen Tadashi's terrible red boar since that first night.

People are like sheep; they get sick if they're left alone.

The next night I wake to him sobbing like he's choking, and I cough and wipe ash off my face. The blankets my sisters and I share are woven red and orange by growing flames. The stars are blotted out; I jump up and run, screaming everyone's names.

Huge figures race over the burning grass, their squeals drowning out the sheep's frantic bleating. Fire licks at one boar's back as he flies past me—I can't tell if he's on fire or creating the blaze—and I smell death on the blast of his coppery breath.

I fall over a body so badly trampled that its intestines look like loose skeins of yarn.

My fingers squelch in bloody mud as I burrow beneath the body. Fire moves so fast over the grassland, sometimes all people can do is lie down and hope it jumps their bodies, hope they survive with only a few burns. Bodies don't burn well, so sometimes herdsmen butcher a sheep or a horse—if they can afford it—and spread the body's entrails over themselves.

Grass all around crackles. Smoke wraps its fingers around my throat.

I pull my scarf over my mouth, grateful for once my little sister makes me wear it to bed. Is she still running, head uncovered and vulnerable? If she's killed by a boar, will her cut-loose spirit be wedded to a demon?

After a small eternity, I dig myself free, hot ashes stinging my palms.

Red rings the opposite horizon like an untimely sunrise. Blackened earth mirrors the night sky, glowing embers as its fading stars.

Then I turn, and there stands Tsus.

His back's ochre bristles are higher than my head, and his ivory tusks curve like hunting bows from his heavy jaws, yellowed teeth jutting between them under those curling lips. They would carve me open like my father's best skinning knife.

I think of my running little sister and my weeping cousin, and the desperation of cornered creatures rises in me. One can flee or hide, but now I can't do either. "Why do you hate us?"

Are you going to run away, day and night girl?

His words should rattle like spears or crack like thunder for all the destruction he's brought. Instead, I lean forward to hear, not sure if my ears or my mind is responsible for catching his quiet voice.

"The High Plains shaman will drive you back across the narrow sea to Akagi's forests."

Tsus shrills, and beneath it I hear brittle laughter. *I ground the shaman's guts and bones down to feed next year's seeds. No one will drive me anywhere I do not wish to go.*

His laugh makes me angry. I flush; the white patches on my face are probably growing pink, which makes me angrier.

"You deserved to be bound by Akagi's greatest shaman for all the sorrow you've created, all the families you've broken, and all the death you've caused. Maybe he'll even come back from the grave and bind you again for your insolence. The world will balance itself. If you do enough evil, that good man will turn away from his next life to stop you."

The certainty of him coldly listening makes me stammer to a halt.

I don't know who you speak of. Whomever he is, he is already in his next life and he certainly never bound me. Consider that, day and night girl.

With a horrible scream, he charges. I panic and stupidly look into his eyes. I know what I will see, but I can't help myself. I scream as well, as if we are locked together in some sick, painful coupling. Him with his bitter indifference and me with all my fear and hate.

My uncle finds me a day later, barely conscious and sick beneath a coat of ash. Aside from a few burns, I'm untouched, but my bones feel beaten. They tell me my little sister was trampled.

Uncle says, "Pity it was her, when she might've married and done her family good."

I spit at him, and he cuffs me.

Later, Mother and I prepare her body for the pyre. As I comb her hair, my hand begins to shake so badly, I have to stop. If I had stayed with her, maybe she wouldn't have run into harm's way.

The ewes begin to starve with nothing but burned grass to eat. Oldest cousin and I carry the stronger lambs who might survive and have bearing years ahead. The rest who stumble and collapse, pitifully bleating, we butcher. The autumn will be hard and the winter harder. We'll need the meat.

We come across a town of blackened stone. The gates crumble as Father, oldest cousin and I enter. The oasis in the centre is choked with ash, which we could skim clean. Near buildings are curled bodies like unborn infants carved of charcoal. Oldest cousin's breathing is rough and noisy. Then a low bellow makes him scream and bolt.

Father finds a wounded water buffalo trapped between buildings. I go look for oldest cousin, wishing I could curse him with long, flaccid goat ears.

"Leave me alone," he says, when I find him.

"I need someone to help me with the sheep."

He shakes his head. "No, you don't."

Sighing, I squat beside him. "Fine. I need someone who's also seen those black eyes."

His laugh is like a crow's. "You don't need anyone, Khulan. Did you ever really see him, or did you just say that to make me feel better?"

"I did more than see him. He nearly trampled me during the fire. I heard him speak." I hear oldest cousin swallow. "He said that Tadashi had never bound him."

"Voice of Wind, do you think that's true? Even the greatest Akagi shaman in history couldn't bind him? What can we do against that?"

"I don't know, but will you help me?"

He stares at the soot between his feet. "I—I can't, Khulan. When he looks out of the fire, he peels me open and turns me inside out like a fresh lamb hide. I hate it, and I hate him, but..." His voice drops. "Mostly I hate me. Then I hate everyone who sits around the fire like nothing's happening."

My stomach sours, and the idea that my cousin might be transformed one day into a boar opens in my mind like a sickly blossom. I grab his clammy hand, but I don't know what to say, so we stand quietly as a breeze plucks at our clothes and my embroidered scarf.

A windstorm kicks up so much ash that we're forced to pitch camp near the dead town. No one can see more than a stride or two ahead.

I march out to feed our goats, squinting miserably. They crowd my legs, bleating and butting into my knees. None of them picks up any of the hay I drop, then they bolt to the far end of the pen.

Out of the gritty blast steps Tsus, ash blowing up from his snout. Papery dust clots on his fur, and I try not to imagine why. I want to run, screaming, to warn the camp, but he would trample me before I made it a dozen steps.

"Go away! You've done enough damage. Can't you just leave us in peace?"

Men took me and locked me in a temple for my 'purity'. Instead, I began to die until I found a way to be free. So why should I care about your peace? None of you have cared about mine.

"What do you mean? My family, my people have never done anything to you." I shiver, despite the summer heat. I've forgotten how his quiet voice is like a poem leaking from a corpse's mouth. If the powerful Tadashi couldn't bind this creature, how would I? Perhaps Tsus is what killed Tadashi in the end, so that the boars were never completely sealed.

Think about what you will do next time we meet, day and night girl. A third meeting is lucky, but a fourth will mean your death. His voice is so close, it's as if we're pressed together skin-to-skin, heartbeat to heartbeat.

My knees fold, and I kneel in the goat pen shuddering until I realise he's vanished.

Only later, when I'm lying in bed, do I pick at his words like pulling out bad stitching. Four is only an unlucky number for Southern and Akagi people. Strange that an evil spirit would care about auspicious numbers.

One hot, late autumn day, oldest sister rides into camp. She dismounts, pulls out a pair of shears, and begins to cut—snip, snip, snip—her long hair in front of the whole camp. She crops it so close to her scalp that it looks like black fuzz. The glossy black lengths she leaves by her horse, then she wordlessly walks into our tent.

Her husband comes boiling into camp a week later, furiously demanding his bride gifts returned. Father drags oldest sister out and points to her bald head. No one mentions that with all the dead sheep, we can't afford to refund the bride price he paid. The rest of the day she sits in our tent, unmoving.

That night I reach across to touch her arm. "I missed you."

"Are Mother and Father going to marry you off too, so everyone can have more food?" Each word is a piece of flint.

"No, I don't think so. I don't want to marry anyway."

"So, you wouldn't be willing to do it for the family?"

"No one would want me." My lungs hurt.

She finally says, "Your marks *have* gotten worse."

My eyes burn, and I nearly yell at her. Then, inexplicably, my arms feel the weight and warmth of the spring lamb who died in my lap yesterday, too thin and ragged to keep breathing, and all I can say is, "I know."

Everything in my world is tearing itself apart.

I scoot closer and put my arms around her. Then she talks, weaving a terrible tapestry in a cool voice that belies the tears running down her cheeks. I want to kick her husband in the gut and hope his intestines burst.

In the morning, I wait until everyone else has risen, and I wash my face last.

Over the bowl of water, I touch the encroaching white around my mouth and eyes. My skin looks like a mask splitting over my own skull, and a tear spoils the watery mirror.

Oldest sister pushes through the yurt door and stops as I duck my head, wipe my face. Then she kneels beside me, her brutally shorn head hidden under a lovely golden scarf, and hesitantly hugs me.

"I'm sorry, Khulan."

Our family treks north even in the face of winter. At least on the high steppe a little grass still grows, and maybe not so many goats and lambs will die. Father gambles well, and we lose less; we know because we hear horrors about the winter from friends and distant cousins who stayed in the southern, fire-ravaged plains.

Father has us fix as large a meal as we can, and the distant cousins visit again. He makes me sit beside him instead of Mother. He talks animatedly, but the cousins watch me like they're weighing goat meat at the market. Then the young one beside his father grimaces.

"I can't do it," he says.

The reason for their visit crashes down on my head, and I jump to my feet. "I never asked you to, little shit-eating worm."

After I run off, oldest sister finds me in our tent and sits beside me. She takes my hand and squeezes it at last.

"Better not to ever marry."

She's right. Of course, she's absolutely right. If only I could convince the ugly fire in my heart.

When we feed the goats, oldest cousin grins at me. "He was skinny like a worm. My brother and I got in trouble for laughing about it later."

But he isn't laughing when he shakes me out of a sound sleep three nights later. For a bleary minute, I'm confused and mad that he's in the girls' tent. Finally, his frantic words sink past my ears.

"The red boar's coming. I can feel him. Voice of Wind, I can feel his eyes."

Panic wakes me up fast.

"Please," oldest cousin's voice shakes. "Please, do something, Khulan."

I walk into the cold, spring air like I have any kind of a plan, anything to keep Tsus from killing me and my family. Our third meeting might be lucky, he'd said, but the fourth would be death. Did that mean he'd spare me, and we could live on borrowed time until he found us one more time?

In the pre-dawn cold, I stand shivering on a hummock. What can I do that others have not tried, that the greatest shaman did not try? I am tired of running and being afraid.

I unwrap my hair and let it fall, black and white, whispering against the backs of my thighs. I decide I won't wait for a fourth meeting. This time, I will stop Tsus or I will die like Tadashi. A shaman helps the unkind world find balance.

The ground groans under his heavy hooves, and his breath billows white from the furnace in his belly. His tusks glint in the faint starlight, and the smell of men's terror, shit and old blood rolls off of him.

"I have a question for you," I say, before his eerie voice can rattle me. "You said people locked you in a temple until you began to die. But those people are long dead now. How did we disturb you?"

How have you not? Your fear and hatred for me has only grown since the moment I stepped into the world, and when my power was unveiled, men hated and feared me even more. What they cannot control, they will destroy. But I will not be chained. I cannot be driven away. I have become the dark mirror of their hearts.

Despair makes me sick. If this is true, no wonder Tadashi failed.

Look at me, day and night girl, and tell me you do not fear or hate me.

I swallow painfully. "I can't. Because I do. I see myself in you." I slide one foot then another forward in the dew wet grass. "But you said you became this way. If you 'became,' then you were not always reflecting our worst."

Solve the riddle then. What was I?

His disgust draws across my skin like an edge of broken glass. What riddle is he talking about? My mouth is dry as autumn grass while I frantically stretch my time, thinking out loud.

"I heard the most powerful shaman ever known was born in Akagi and subdued all of its wild boars, but you said you were never bound. Your power was unveiled later, not at first. You know us, and someone tried to drive you away, so you must have lived among people."

Then the answer quivers in my mind, and I gape at it.

"Because… you are Tadashi Daito."

The giant boar groans like a breaking leg, then he collapses forward into the wet grass. A hot gust of ash hits my face, and I cough, waving a hand. When the air doesn't sting my eyes anymore, I can see a man kneeling where the bloody boar stood. He cocks his head, black eyes glittering like a carrion bird's. Maybe some curses are not so easily broken.

I cautiously sink down in the cold grass facing him and hug my scarf around my shoulders. "What happened to you?"

Unlike most men's hair, his is unbound and falls over his shoulder, bright as bitter berries and catching hints of copper light like fire viewed through glass.

"I bent all the Akagi warlords to my will, and the people were glad for it, but they would not step on my shadow. I was a monster—their monster—left with only bitter, broken men for company. Fear on one side and hatred on the other. So, I cursed the warlords, took away their voices, and made them animals. But in cursing them, I also cursed myself." He looks sideways at me, a little sadly but also with a glimmer of the alien blackness. "Now they are free too. I can't say what they'll do, but I think it will be less harm than they did under my hand."

Maybe he's waiting to see if I'm afraid.

I'm not anymore, though I am irritated. "Two hundred years of peace is nothing to wag a rat's tail at, but you're coming with me to find them now. I'm holding you responsible for dumping a bunch of pig warlords into my homeland."

He chuckles. "Fair enough."

"Why did you call me 'day and night girl'?"

Considering, he takes my bleached hand lightly, as if asking permission. "Even as I was, perhaps because of what I am, I see what people try to ruin. Your hand is a sunlit cloud, the harvest moon. Your arm is the night sky, rich earth in summer. Do not let others steal what is lovely." He turns his head strangely; there's still something of a wild creature in his movements. "You and I have been called many names, most of which only describe a small part of us. But you've finally called me by a true name. Would you tell me yours?"

I grimace and shift. It's one thing to save the land's most powerful shaman. It's quite another to tell him you're named after a wild ass.

"If… you don't wish to," he says softly, "I understand."

"No, it's fine! It's just—Oh, goat farts. It's Khulan."

He coughs, then a laugh bursts out, from the belly and almost completely human in the growing glow of dawn.

The Pearls That Were His Eyes

Featured in Issue #75

…Jennifer R Donohue

Clary read the contract and tried to be thorough as the legalese swam in front of her eyes. After years of working protections, blessing openings, and, yes, talking to the dead, it was clear that when people somehow found out witches existed, they hired them. And nobody wanted it known that witches had been used, the witches especially.

She finally cleared her throat. Ferdinand looked up at her, eyes bright in his scruffy red face. "Is this… dollar amount correct?" she asked.

Mr Rankin nodded. "It is. We'll pay you a million dollars. Provided your work is what helps us with our particular problem."

"And if it isn't?"

"Half a million, no bonus. I'm not certain what services such as these usually cost, but we did exhaust other methods before reaching this juncture. I don't understand the lack of response to our ad. All we need is a door opened."

They're probably smarter than me, she wanted to say. She did not. They were probably just less broke than her. His gaze made Clary very aware of her tattoos, her nose stud. He seemed to be trying not to look at Ferdinand, who was lying down next to her chair, panting happily, his tail occasionally thumping on the thick, plush carpet.

"I kind of thought we'd come to the wrong place," Clary said. In addition to her purse, she carried a leather satchel full of tools. Blessed chalk, pennyroyal, acacia thorns and mistletoe. Candles. A strand of Polish amber around her neck. Warding circles saved on her tablet, if her go-to didn't seem sufficient. Ferdinand's leash looped on her wrist.

Mr Rankin gave a plummy chuckle, and Clary thought of polo ponies and boat shoes. "I'll bet you did. We don't look at all like a company in the habit of hiring witches, do we?" She didn't quite know what the company was; the building was an old, meticulously kept brownstone, not offices in a skyscraper. He didn't even have pens on his desk.

"Not really." She wished something other than "witch" had been settled upon as the catchall term for people like her. It wasn't incorrect, nor was it precisely correct. Though Clary supposed she didn't call herself anything; she just was.

"Is the amount sufficient?" Mr Rankin asked, his impatience carefully masked.

The situation was dreadful, and also fascinating, though she didn't feel threatened. The protection knot tattooed on the inside of her wrist neither warmed nor itched. "Just a few questions," she said.

Mr Rankin blinked at her. It was the first time she'd gone off script, apparently. She wondered if any other applicants had come at all, or if they'd skimmed over the ad or turned away at their bus stop, at the corner, at the front steps. "What is it?"

"The owner of the door you can't open. How did he pass?"

"Does it matter?"

"It's good for me to know, before I do anything." If he'd been murdered, she'd leave. If it was a car accident, she'd leave. If he was very old, or if he'd been ill, it was all right. The danger, to herself or beyond herself, came from the anger of the dead, those who had been torn away abruptly. Like when a poster was torn off a wall and the taped-up corners remained.

"The elder Mr Rankin was in his eighties. He caught pneumonia five years ago, and it never really left him. He passed two years ago this August."

"Your father?"

His posture tightened just a little, across the shoulders, in his jaw. "Yes. My father."

"Do you know what's inside the room?"

"I do not."

She couldn't speak for a moment, planning her words carefully. "I must be left alone to do this, you understand? It might be dangerous for you otherwise." Not to mention deeply unsettling, to do spellwork in front of somebody uninitiated.

"I don't like it. But I understand."

She signed. Mr. Rankin signed. Clary tucked her copy of the contract into her purse.

Mr Rankin took them, Ferdinand's tags jangling, through smoke-painted walls, edged with dark-stained wood, to a door of equally dark wood, brass bound. "Is it always dogs?" Mr Rankin asked. "I'm sure it's rude for me to ask, I apologise."

"It isn't always dogs, no," Clary said. Most people who did spellwork, whether it was just personal charms or larger rituals, had a dog. Maybe they could be considered familiars but, like the word witch, that wasn't really part of Clary's personal lexicon. Ferdinand grounded her, helped her feel safe and protected.

Mr Rankin leaned into the door's retinal scan and it beeped open. Not the special door yet, then. She was wildly curious about its contents, fighting with herself every time she took a step closer to it. She wanted very much to leave. The revealed stairway was wrought iron, and a thrum went up Clary's spine when she stepped onto it. Ferdinand hesitated a moment then lowered his muzzle to sniff before continuing. The walls were papered green, very green, and she wondered if it was the kind of antique wallpaper that was dyed with arsenic. There was a pattern to the paper, but not a large one, and her eye couldn't quite catch it as she followed along with Mr Rankin. The light here was different as well, a yellow subterranean glow, versus the blue white LED in the rest of the building.

The air cooled as they descended, Mr Rankin in the lead. The floor, when they reached it, was concrete. Slightly gritty, somewhat damp. Clary couldn't tell just at a guess how far below street level they were. They went through several rooms, mostly empty, sometimes stacked with desks or chairs. But no dust anywhere, no cobwebs. A certain indistinct charge to the air. And then they came to another locked door, another retinal scan. "It's just inside here," he said. All these layers of security were unsettling.

The door beeped and swung open, and the resulting room was so like the office they'd started in that Clary felt a moment of disorientation. A tremendous desk and leather chairs so expensive and well-made that their soft lustre exuded expense, both in the making and in whatever animal had given its life for them because it seemed as though it could be no mere cow. Files were on this desk, and wooden card catalogue-style drawers, brass knobbed, lined the walls. And in those walls, there was another dark wood door. Brass bound. Retinal scan. The brass had etchings in it, though, and even from across the room Clary's wrist tattoo itched.

"That's the door then," she said quietly, her head tilted. There was a ringing in her ears, which would be ignorable as the fluorescent hum in another place, but these weren't fluorescent lights. This wasn't another place.

"It is. Only my father's retinal scan would open it. I've had my retinas replaced with cloned copies of his, which work in the other doors we just came through, but not this one." Clary turned to look at him. "There's a fingerprint scanner here as well, which also won't work with his fingerprints laid over another person's. We've tried just a cloned finger, with artificial circulation—still nothing."

"Cloned from…" The others must have asked better questions before now. She'd tried to think of better questions before now. Cloned body parts. A minnow shiver in her belly. She ought to have grasped more fully, and much earlier, that Mr Rankin did not seem affected by his father's death and was only consumed by the need to open this last door. But a person's public face and private one could be so different. Ferd nudged her hand. She stroked his head and held one of his ears briefly.

"He left any number of cells… around." Mr Rankin gestured in the air. "With cloning technology and 3D printing what it is, we could rebuild him wholesale if we needed to. But we only tried the parts for the locks, and they didn't work." He turned, saw the look on her face, and sighed. "We only went the body parts route after the security expert declared it impossible, unless he drilled through the door, like breaking into an old bank vault. To do so would almost certainly destroy the contents."

"I see," she said. There was no computer, but there was an old-fashioned typewriter with a box of envelopes beside it. Some chewed pencils resided with expensive looking pens in a tray on the desk. A leather desk chair, the arms worn pale. A brown velvet wingback chair nestled into the closest corner, its arms also worn. The floor was concrete, just like the previous basement rooms, but there were silver and blue threaded oriental rugs littering the space, white tasselled. On the card catalogue, some of the brass knobs were shinier than others. "He spent a lot of time here?"

"This is where he spent the most time outside of his home. I won't give you access to his home."

She didn't want to do this. But a million dollars meant health insurance, and her student debt and credit card debt wiped out. She could move out of the city, get a little house someplace safe, and have a garden. Clary took a deep breath, tried to calm down and think. She'd signed the contract. She was obligated now and felt that keenly. "This should do. And something he wrote on or communicated with—a notebook, a shopping list, something."

"Oh, of course. We had a box of such items curated in anticipation of this request. It's beside the desk."

The itching in her wrist calmed down. She went to look at the etchings on the door, which seemed oddly standard, in fact. Variations on the Keys of Solomon with some other flavour mixed in, personal or familial, Clary couldn't yet say. Maybe she'd never know. Something about the dark and gummy wood bothered her, and she didn't want to touch it without certain precautions that she had not yet taken, and not in front of Mr Rankin. The room smelled like sandalwood, she realised. Sandalwood and old vanilla and something else. Basement damp, but that was to be expected. Something acrid. Sulphur? Her mind kept trying to match it up, and kept saying it couldn't, with the wards on the door.

Keeping something out or keeping something in?

But Mr Rankin was talking to her. "I'm sorry?" Clary said.

Mr Rankin looked at her, looked at the dog. "I hope we've provided supplies to your satisfaction."

"I'm sure you've done fine," she said, also with an eye on Ferdinand. He wasn't frightened, but he was on alert, and he looked from the door to her and back again. He had his nose in the air, and his tail up.

"You can call me at this number, and I'll come back down immediately with anything you need," he said, handing her a business card. "Barring that, call when the door is open and the room beyond is safe to view."

"All right." She took the card.

Mr Rankin withdrew and Clary unsnapped Ferdinand's leash. He sniffed about the perimeter of the room, and stood stock-still in front of the door, whining quietly.

"I know, Ferd," she said. "But it's okay, isn't it?" He advanced and sniffed the door audibly for several moments without touching it, as she laid out the contents of her satchel. Eventually he sneezed twice, then came over and nosed her neck. "Okay then."

She drew the inner circle in chalk first—the one for the belongings of the deceased—which was designed centuries ago to keep whatever was in it, in it, no exceptions. Then she inspected the box by the desk: a mustard yellow cardigan, a marbled composition notebook, nothing written on the cover, but full of closely pencilled script from cover to cover.

Instead of a comb or a brush, there was a strange square vessel, like a medical specimen bottle combined with a fish tank, and Clary grimaced as she bent down to look at a pair of eyes floating within. Either they'd been a pale blue, or they didn't really colourise properly when they were printed. The optic nerves were hooked up to something that made about as much noise as a fish tank filter, and she couldn't say what she thought the liquid was. "Thanks, Rankin," she muttered. Ferdinand sniffed stiffly toward the eyes then backed off, ears folded to the sides.

Clary folded the cardigan and laid it in the middle of the circle, then placed the notebook on top of it. She gingerly picked up the eye tank and carried it over, her witch's knot itching the entire time, the hair on the back of her neck struggling to stand. Ferdinand grunted at her and backed out of the way. The objects were set, and she poured out a spiral of sea salt.

She always felt a thrill of anticipation when preparing like this, and whatever energy was in the room fed into that thrill. She didn't get the impression that this Mr Rankin had been a bad man, though not necessarily a good one either. It could just be that he tried his best. Or it could be he did something terrible that he then spent the rest of his days atoning for.

"Where should the candles go?" she asked Ferdinand, and he walked one by one to different places in the room, not stopping at four for once—the cardinal directions—but adding a fifth and a sixth at odd angles. "This is new." He cocked his head at her and barked once, softly. He'd returned to his loose posture, though, ears up, tail wagging periodically. His mouth tightened if he looked at the eyes, but he solved that by not looking at the eyes. The lit candles, cedar scented, brightened up the space, made it feel more complete.

Clary set up the big primary Seal of Solomon, altered in her own way with some additional symbols that spoke to her, stopping a couple of times to look at the etchings on the door again. This time she did touch the wood, only to find it drier than it looked. Drier than a wood door in a basement should be, anyway. The chalk had, at times, been smeary on the damp concrete. She stood there awhile looking at the brass etchings on the door, then brushed her fingertips along them, trying to unfocus herself and think without thinking, to let thoughts or impulses surface. She took the chalk and drew a half circle coming out from the door, as though she were chalking a doormat, and copied the symbols at the edges too—a crescent moon, some hooked geometric things she thought might be Enochian—before laying more salt. "Music?" she asked Ferdinand, who flicked his ears. She shrugged too. She laid herbs outside the salt, following the same lines.

She stood in the big circle, looked at the eyes, and called out to Mr Rankin. Some people did this out loud in varying languages—Latin or German or French or any hundreds of others. There were magical traditions all over the world.

In Kenya, in Laos, in Poland, and in nearly every modern case, individuals had their own way, forging brief apprentices or partnerships, swapping power for power, splitting off and continuing alone again. Clary did not call out loud. She looked at the eyes and then her own rolled back and she spread her arms, letting the power thrum up her spine to her crown, until it felt as though the top of her head had opened up to allow the cosmos access. She felt the dry autumn leaves rustle of a response.

The presence drew back sharply when she suggested the door, then returned, power growing in front of her like a kindling fire. She tilted her head back down, looked forward; the eyes in the tank had moved to look up at her. Clary suggested the door again. The eyes, lacking lids, moved toward the door and looked at her again. She nodded, stepped forward through the circles to pick up the tank. Ferdinand let out a high-pitched whistle through his nose. Clary stopped. "Is it okay?" she asked him. Ferdinand licked his lips and backed up three steps, but that was it.

There was something the older Mr Rankin worried about, something he wanted protected from. His son? The world at large? It was hard to tell. The pages of his notebook ruffled, but she hadn't the knack for either Ouija boards or automatic writing. The feeling of that much Other coursing through her, under her skin, was just too much; the wrong voltage through a connection would damage it after very little time.

"You feel trapped?" Clary asked out loud. No, that wasn't it. Close. "Something is trapped?" Better. "You trapped it? Your son trapped it? Your son wants it." Yes, Rankin wants it. But who trapped it wasn't the point. "What happens if I set it free?" A brief feeling of peace. He hadn't meant to die and leave whatever was there still locked away. He'd meant to free it himself, but something had prevented him.

"All right then." Ferdinand relaxed again, his tail wagging just a little bit. He still didn't like the door, or what was behind it, but he was okay with the eyes. Clary felt she was right to have warded the floor even more. She'd never worked a summoning herself but knew people did regularly. They all had their own reasons, and results varied. She held the eye tank out to the retinal scan, and, without really activating, the scan beeped. In response, the door popped ajar.

The light inside the warded door was liquid amber, darker than the beads strung around Clary's neck. The eyes, Mr Rankin, were happy—happy and anticipatory—and Clary sort of nudged at the door until it reached the point where it swung the rest of the way open itself. She saw there, chained in silver, why the elder Mr Rankin would have had his workspace in the basement. The beautiful, silver-chained reason he was so uneasy, and so distrustful of his son.

What the being was exactly, Clary was not qualified to say. Not at a glance. It was luminous, large eyed, horned, with long, long hair and extra-jointed fingers, all hips and curves and angles. The silver didn't seem to hurt it exactly, but it, and the black hammered runes, were restrictive. Otherwise Clary thought even she could physically break those bonds.

"How?" she asked the eyes, or the being before her. She couldn't look at it or look away. Every angel is terrible, she thought, but maybe that wasn't quite the right line. And this wasn't quite an angel. Demon? Something else from beyond the firelight? The words came to her, and she mouthed them and immediately forgot them, like trying to read in a dream. The silver chains fell away and the thing looked at her with its bright liquid eyes and started to cross the room.

The amber beads on Clary's necklace snapped one after the other, like popcorn kernels, sticky sap running down her collarbones, and Ferdinand was barking, barking, and Mr Rankin's eyes were thrumming in their tank, turned fully to the being, which stopped at the threshold of the open door in front of where the salt started, and cocked its head impossibly far, like an owl, first one way and then the other. It crouched to the floor and seemed to write something there, brought a hand to its mouth and bit its thumb. The blood that dripped was not black, not red, not gold, but it seemed like all those things, and then the smell was strong again, like sulphur and like honeysuckles and like low tide, and then the being was gone. No puff of smoke, no flash of light, just gone like it was never there to begin with, leaving the air all the clearer for it.

Clary stumbled and set the eyes on the desk before she dropped them. She was so bone weary she could lie on the pile of oriental rugs and sleep for a week, no matter what she'd just seen or felt. Ferdinand nosed her, and she rubbed her hands over his scruffy fur, then bent and hugged him to her, feeling his heart through her breastbone. The candles were all out, air laden with the smell of spent smoke and cooling wax. "Let's clean up," she murmured.

It didn't take long, even with her stumbling and Ferdinand leaning into her. The chalk dissipated with the barest suggestion of a brushing, which she had a bundle of straw and sage for. The herbs and salt crumbled away into nothing. Clary could still see those burning bright eyes, eyes beyond human conception and understanding. And Mr Rankin's eyes watched her still, though she could tell he was tired too. There was something else he wanted to tell her. He wanted her to go into that room.

Like a sleepwalker, she crossed the threshold hesitantly, rosary clutched in her left hand, made from Jerusalem olive wood. The room was many drawered like a bank vault, and the pile of silver on the floor had not gone away on its own, but Mr Rankin wasn't concerned with that, so Clary ignored it. One of the drawers wiggled just a little as she drew near, the way the composition notebook had, and Clary pulled it open. In it was a small, black, leather bound book with silver chasing on the cover that matched the door. She had just enough time to shove it in her pocket and go back into the office before she heard the chiming of the outer locks.

She went to the outer room as Mr Rankin swung the door shut behind him. "It's all yours," she said. Ferdinand stood between them and his tail was not wagging. She buckled up her satchel and shouldered it, along with her purse.

After the chained being, she was hungry to look at another human, but her eyes slid off the younger Mr Rankin, her skin electric with an aversion she couldn't ignore for much longer.

"I can see that." He pulled out his phone, tapped a few times, and then dropped it into his shirt pocket again. "The money is being transferred to your account as we speak. You're responsible for claiming your own taxes, of course."

"Thank you," she said. The silver didn't look like chains anymore, she thought. It looked like a pile of coins. He brushed past her, moving to the silver and the drawers. "I'll see myself out, then," Clary said, but he gave no indication of remembering she existed. "Come on, Ferd."

The walk back through the basement rooms seemed longer, darker, emptier. She kept looking over her shoulder, but of course Mr Rankin wasn't behind her. Ferdinand would warn her long before he was within arm's reach, at any rate. Finally, though, they were out of the yellow light, back through the green wallpapered stairwell.

Nobody in the brownstone would even look at her, or Ferdinand, as they searched for the front door, wandering for what seemed like miles on all that plush carpet but probably only taking three minutes. Once they were in the sunlight again, Clary could have sat on the front steps, hugged Ferd to her, and wept. Her phone chimed, and she pulled it out mechanically, right in the middle of the sidewalk. It was her bank, reporting a suspicious transaction, and she looked at it long enough that the screen went back to sleep. A million dollars to start the rest of her life with. And whatever was in old Mr Rankin's black book. She should probably burn it.

She wouldn't burn it.

My Name is Draco

Featured in Issue #76

…Tara Campbell

Greetings, fellow travellers down the path of healing. My name is Draco, and I am a knightoholic. It has been almost two years since I've eaten a man.

Thank you, fellow dragons, you are too kind. Each and every one of us in this cave tonight knows how difficult this journey is. Yes, humans are our traditional fare, but I was consuming them rather more often than was necessary or wise. I gobbled them up day and night (no pun intended). And when I wasn't eating them I was thinking about them: raw, roasted, fried, boiled in oil, kebab, the possibilities are—were—endless. I only regret that I didn't seek help soon enough. Had I done so, all of my subsequent problems might have been avoided.

My obsession with knights began to affect my relationships. You know this dynamic well, fellow dragons. Friends stopped going out to eat with me, said I couldn't hunt like a normal beast, complained that I wouldn't leave any for them. My wife began to lose interest in me—believe it or not, I was almost two tons overweight at that time. My low point came when she began talking about a wyvern on her project team at work, rather more than I found agreeable. That was it, I decided. That's when I had to start treating my knight addiction seriously. I couldn't lose Penelope.

I was no longer in control, dear seekers of wellness, but I knew I had to do something. I devised a plan to cut down on humans by eating what *they* ate instead. It seemed a sound strategy. We've all observed how they diet: instead of eating the chicken or the cow, they eat more corn or salad. However, I did not, as they say, think it through. I mean, how svelte is all that corn actually making them? As I've mentioned, I was not in my best state of mind.

I began to observe what knights ate. I watched revellers at the Solstice Feast, saw them succumb to gluttony with their chickens and roasts and potatoes and wine and ale. Despite the music and merriment, regardless of the fragrance of roasted boar, I was initially most despondent. Nothing on their menu was new to me, I'd eaten all of those animals before, and I was still craving the flesh of the knights themselves.

Ah, but then I asked myself the fateful question: what were they drinking? I watched them lift silver tankards of ale up to their mouthfur, slake their thirst, them slam their mugs back down on the tables, again and again. Well, drink was something I hadn't thought of before, so focused on food was I. Reinvigorated with hope, I swooped down and carried off two barrels of their finest ale. You should have seen their faces! Naturally, they all thought I was coming for them, and when I went for the barrels they froze with shock. The irony was not lost on me: with their reaction to my attempt to stop eating them, I could have scooped them up in my maw like cows off a hillside.

But no, I didn't indulge in mass carnage; and yet, I had a delightful evening back at my lair. I know it is unwise to glorify our addictions, but—have any of you tried ale? Can you understand the release, the escape? The sense of utter physical and emotional weightlessness? Well, I'm ashamed to say, I even pressed Penelope to try some. She hated it. She's a far wiser dragon than I.

A few days later I winged over to the castle to crash a knighthood ceremony, and what did I see—two barrels of ale at the foot of the drawbridge, branded with a silhouette of a dragon. *Thank you very much, gentlemen*, I said to myself, *and a good night to you all.*

A few days after that I made my way toward a village wedding, fancying a peck of pauper, and once again, a gift of ale awaited me. They'd begun to catch on, . they They knew they could save their skins by putting a couple of barrels outside the feast for me.

From then on, for every celebration—weddings, birthdays, christenings, anniversaries—the villagers always made sure to leave a couple of casks out for me. Over the months, the image on the barrels began to look more and more like me. One month, it was no longer a brand, but hand-drawn. Another month they reshaped the wings to match mine (more bat-like), then added the exact number of horns on my snout (three). After that, they began to colour it in, using daubs of blue, green, and white paint to capture the sheen of my scales.

I must admit, I rather liked their work. I began to linger when I picked up my barrels, circling overhead longer than necessary, or landing and pretending to sniff and inspect the barrels before I carried them off. They began to watch from the edge of the field when I landed—only a few at first, but a larger crowd gathered each time.

I developed a habit of drinking one barrel on site before carrying the second one off. I'd begun to feel bad about demolishing the decorated barrels, so I learned to pierce the end with a claw and empty the contents into my mouth. Back at my lair I kept a growing collection of these artworks. Penelope loathed the lingering scent of ale, but even she admired the craftsmanship of the casks. I swore her to secrecy, however, and allowed no other dragon to see my collection, lest anyone should divine the source of my burgeoning riches.

Some brave souls began to bring out a mug and a stool when I arrived, getting comfortable as I prolonged my stay. Then a table appeared. And another. And another, and a tent for shade, until by the end of the year, a whole festival site had sprung up around the field where I would land.

I fell into a rhythm of appearing twice a month. Couples began to arrange marriages around my appearances; children waited to celebrate their birthdays until I arrived. And then one day—pardon me if I become a little emotional here—one day I caught wind of a large celebration as I neared the village, but couldn't divine the occasion. It was not yet time for a Solstice event, but looked to be almost as elaborate. When I landed, I found—it still brings a tear to my eye to think on it—it was a celebration just for me!

Banners with my likeness fluttered in a ring around my field. Children ran about holding up straw puppets of me—crudely made, but I could tell they had tried as best they could. Within minutes of my arrival, the stoutest men of the village rolled out a replica of me, three times as tall as any of them, made entirely out of wood. Its mighty wings were unfurled to their full, glorious span, and its head tilted up toward the heavens. Each scale was painstakingly painted blue, green, or white, and they were interspersed with metal shingles to reflect the blaze of the sun. It was, simply put, a masterpiece.

My heart, dear compatriots, my heart…

Pardon my tears, I simply cannot think back on it without becoming sentimental. Because oh, fellow dragons, it was not merely a statue, some dead, blank effigy. No. When the villagers grasped the wings and pumped them up and down, rich golden ale came spouting out of the dragon's upturned mouth!

They had designed this dragon just for me, and filled it with the substance dearest to me. They pumped my replica's wings, and I dipped my head into the fountain of ale for a long, heady drink. That they would do this for me, until recently their most dread foe—I could barely contain myself. Knowing I would crush them if I remained on the ground, I launched into the sky and flew loops in the heavens. I could hear the applause as I wheeled and curved, and their cheers were caresses on every inch of my body.

I gambolled in the air until I had calmed enough to avoid smashing them with happiness. I circled and settled and tried to hold myself as still as possible. In that moment, I could think of nothing more delightful than to have one of these human creatures put a hand on my scales. I'd seen them do this to each other, and to other creatures toward which they felt tenderness, and I felt that this gesture, this touch, would be the crowning moment of my connection to every human in this village.

And oh, when I saw the look in one young mother's eye, I knew she understood. We had made an unspoken connection, mind to mind, confident that we would forge a new path in human-dragon relations. With one outstretched hand, she would start a new chapter in both of our histories.

And she did reach out, in a way I could never have imagined. Slowly, steadily, she raised her baby—yes, her own progeny—in my direction. The child gently pedalled its feet and cooed in its mother's hands, stretching its pudgy fingers out toward my snout. My nostrils flared, drinking in the babe's sweet, warm scent. I blinked in disbelief of the trust and tenderness these two humans were showing me.

Until the worst imaginable thing happened. Quite without any conscious planning on my part, my tongue dashed out between my teeth, its two forks acting as twin demons independent of my control, scooping the baby out of its mother's hands, and carrying the wriggling child back toward my mouth. I opened wide to keep the baby from shredding to bits on my razor-sharp teeth; then, instinctively, my jaw clamped shut upon the baby inside my mouth. It squirmed upon my tongue and kicked against the roof of my mouth, and now when I think back on it, I shudder to think how tightly I had to clench my teeth together to keep them from doing their natural work.

When I realised what was happening, I gasped, which only drew the infant further back toward my throat. Fortunately, I immediately recovered and spat, and the child came tumbling out onto the grass, slimy but whole, red-faced, wailing and thrashing. Alive.

My throat was agitated by my near-choking experience. I tried to turn away, concerned that my coughing might produce a flame or two. But there was nowhere to turn; I was surrounded by villagers. I raised my head and coughed, igniting one of the straw effigies the children had made of me. I wheeled and coughed again, this time setting one of the beautiful, hand-stitched dragon flags aflame. As I turned yet again, I felt villagers tumbling over my thrashing tail. The humans began to scatter, screaming and cursing, running in all directions. Flames leapt from one flag to another, sending my banners into conflagration. As the smoke thickened, disoriented villagers began running toward me as well as away. I knew I had to fly away to avoid doing any more damage, but I think—I think I might have stepped on one or two humans in my haste to lift off.

I circled once over the field to see if there was anything I could do. Unfortunately, it seems the wind from my wings carried embers from the field fire onto a nearby straw roof. The thatch began to smoulder as I turned toward home. Then, I thought with a sudden dread of the contents of the giant dragon-shaped barrel and looked around just in time to see it erupt, with a thunderous boom, into a golden-white ball of flame.

The following day I flew over the village again, hoping. I'll admit, it was not an altruistic visit. I wanted to alleviate the heaviness of my heart with the sight of a village only slightly damaged, perhaps just a scorched field next to an intact settlement.

What I saw instead was a razed shell of a village, with smoke still rising from the blackened expanse of sticks and ash. It was too much to bear.

The following day, I came back to see if there was some way I could apologise and help them rebuild, only to be met by burning arrows and flaming balls of pitch flung by trebuchet: the king's army had gotten involved. They wouldn't have been any match for me, of course, but I didn't have the stomach for battle. I didn't have the stomach for much of anything since, least of all more humans.

There was, needless to say, no Solstice Festival that year. Only the sawing of wood and the crack of hammers rebuilding what was lost. I flew over the village day after day, staying high enough to escape attack, but also too high to lend any assistance. The one bright spot: there were no funerals in the aftermath of the disaster—my worst fears were allayed.

And yet, I have only traded one worry for another. Penelope has become concerned, watching me moping about the lair, withering away on a meagre diet of mountain goats and deer. And meanwhile the knights have become emboldened, riding out on in search parties armed with torches and swords. Penelope has seen them on her flights, daring to come closer to our lair with every outing. They taunt me, and yet, I do not wish to succumb to my addictions. That is why I have come to you tonight, fellow dragons. I seek your guidance on a plan, one that may stave off an even more grave tragedy.

There is to be a royal wedding soon—the king's daughter will marry the prince of the neighbouring land. It will be an elaborate affair, with music and dance, jesters and drink, and feasting by all the king's men. I will not be able to celebrate with them as once I could. It pains me to think of what could have been. The most I can do now is go and try to seek peace—through equilibrium.

Both humans and I have learned a powerful lesson: dragons and ale don't mix. But Penelope is right, : I still require certain things, and if I don't take them in moderation, I will eventually find myself on the path of destruction once again. And, as weddings mark the start of new hopes and dreams, dear dragons, I have come to you for your blessings as I embark on a new plan for healing. I have tried everything, friends. I have even allowed myself to drink of their drink, a substance which made me believe I could counter the laws of nature and heaven above. And so, I believe: if I stick to a steady diet of knights—one per month, say—I'll never have to go back to the barrel again.

What say ye, fellow denizens of air and lair?

The Angles

Featured in Issue #74

...A T Sayre

"One. *At the tone, count five seconds out loud and press the button."*
"One. Two. Three. Four. Five."

The machine beeped in Matthews' ear when he pressed the button. It wasn't loud, but the pitch grated on him. The soulless dark lens in the wall in front of him stared back, unmoved. After a moment the voice continued.

"Two. At the tone, count fourteen seconds out loud and press the button."

A brief pause, then the beep sounded again. "One. Two. Three. Four," Matthews counted, closing his eyes.

"Please keep your eyes open," the machine said.

"What?"

"Please keep your eyes open and face the camera."

Matthews sighed and sat straighter in his chair. "Let me start over. You interrupted me."

"Acknowledged. At the tone, count fourteen seconds out loud and press the button."

He leaned forward on his elbow as he began again, his finger hovering over the red button. It was hard to get comfortable in the small room. It wasn't any larger than a closet, with just the stiff chair and the ledge where the button was in front of the camera lens. The abnormally high ceiling was the only part of the room that kept him from feeling completely boxed in.

He focused on his reflection in the dark glass as he counted. He could see the contours of his brow, cheeks, the tip of his nose, but the rest of his face was a void. It was like his reflection in the glass dome of the cockpit, the bulb at the nose of his snake-like ship. That was where he belonged, strapped down to the inner wall, arms on the armrests, a joystick in each hand. Facing the whole universe beyond the ghostly image of his own reflection.

He cleared the asteroid belt on his way to the angles out by Jupiter. The distant gas giant was a tiny red dot far off in front of him. A wart on his invisible cheek. Just to the left of it was the Milky Way, the mist of billions of fiery orbs cutting down through his face like a scar.

He pulled on the joystick in his left hand and the ship tumbled. The escort drones in front furiously repositioned themselves to match him. He smiled. It was one of the few distractions he had, twisting and twirling, sending the drones into a frantic dance to remain in formation. The passengers and flight crew in the attached compartments behind him never seemed to mind, or at least they never said anything. They probably enjoyed the twirling sky. Not that he would have cared if they did complain. He was the pilot. If he wanted to dance a little to break up the hours of tedium they would just have to deal with it.

"Ain't nobody can tell you what to do out there," Franks said, looking across the table at Matthews with the devilish smirk he got when he was feeling boisterous. "You could fly the whole way backwards if you want. We're in charge in the void. That's our world. Pilots rule. Who else they gonna get who can fly the angles? No one, that's who." He took a long drink and slammed his glass down, making his date jump.

The civilians loved this kind of talk. The brashness of it, the ego. They always crowded around and wanted to be near the pilots, with them. Pilots were the dashing heroes. Pilots were special.

"Admit it, you live for the attention."

"Of course I do!" Franks roared with a laugh. "Who wouldn't? Who complains about being looked up to? Everyone wishes they could be us, live our lives. Wishes they could shoot the angles and come out the other side. We've seen the whole damn universe. And even more than that. They know it's more than anything any of them will ever experience in their safe, mundane lives. The biggest high-powered exec in New York would give up every penny they have to fly in the cockpit just once."

"So, we're living the dream."

Franks grinned wide. "Absolutely. I wouldn't give it up for anything."

Matthews finished counting and pressed the button. Again, the light beep was almost immediate.

"Three. At the tone, count thirty-seven seconds out loud, and press the button."

Jupiter soon grew into a cloudy orb up ahead, about the size of his head. The ship was directly between the gas giant and the distant sun, the planet full and bright. The nav comp locked on to it, dropping a small window with basic targeting data onto the overhead display. He ignored it and looked at the planet. The larger clouds and chaotic storms could be made out across its surface, along with a small dark spot rolling along the equator. Probably Ganymede passing by. The others would be too small to be visible from here.

This was a favourite sight for passengers, and there were a few more hours for them to enjoy it before Matthews would turn on stasis. He angled the ship a few degrees and flew just slightly askew to give the port side a better view. It was easy enough to reposition the thrusters to keep the steady deceleration constant. An old, flashy trick he had mastered years ago.

Matthews stared at a spot just below the distant planet. There was nothing to see there except the empty void. But that was where they were headed. To the angles. They were still too far away for the computers to register them, so nothing showed up on the display. But Matthews could feel them tugging at him from hundreds of thousands of kilometres away. That's where the real piloting happened. He felt his chest getting tight in anticipation.

Travelling between the stars was all about the angles. The curious interplay of the gravitational pull of the sun and the planets against each other created microscopic tears in space. Every planet had them; Mercury just the one, ten among the other inner planets combined, more among the gas giants. Jupiter alone had more than a hundred. But they were innocuous, affecting nothing. Dust, comets, and ships could fly straight through them without even knowing it.

Unless you came at them at exactly the right angle. If you positioned your ship to pass through them just so, down to millimetre precision. Continuously adjusting and repositioning, shifting this way, twisting that, not overshooting, getting it just right. It took an expert hand.

"Six. At the tone, count one hundred forty-five seconds—"

"What happened to four and five?"

The machine stopped. Matthews could hear a slight whir. *"Repeat. Six. At the tone, count one hundred forty-five seconds out loud and press the button."*

He shook his head and waited. The machine was deviating from the standard test by jumping ahead. It made him apprehensive. It was trying to trip him up.

"The department is being forced on this, Matthews," Weiters told him. "You understand that, right?"

Matthews shrugged at his supervisor. "I guess."

"This isn't me. This is coming from the top. These new studies coming out of Luna are pretty bad, and Central can't ignore them anymore. There's too much public outcry. The tests are now compulsory every quarter. No exceptions."

Matthews had always quietly despised Chief Weiters. Most of the pilots did at some level. The man hadn't done more than a year in a cockpit before he had moved behind a desk. He talked like he was on their side, as if he knew what it was to be a true pilot, and maybe he did. But he still wasn't really one of them.

Weiters continued. "I've already had to ground Suarez and Jacobs. I just got Mindoye's results back this morning and she's done too. Not much of a surprise there; she's been out of it for years. This is going to wipe out our whole squad."

Matthews looked at the old-fashioned lamp sitting on Weiters' table. Little specks of dust sparkled in the light directly above the bulb. They were kept aloft in the heated air as they flowed past, appearing and disappearing as they moved in and out of the light.

Franks leaned across the table, his chin just above the lampshade. The thin hairs on his face shone in the light. "You see this new crop of pilots?" he asked.

"Some of them," Matthews replied.

"Fucking useless the whole batch of them." Franks took a long swig from his glass.

"Maybe they're a little green."

"A little? I watched that new kid, whatshisname? Guilfoye. I was behind him in line at the Neptune field the other day and watched him miss the Taurus angle three times before he got it. It was brutal. He'd come full stop, dance around and twist and turn and then just jump at it, so of course he kept missing. I felt embarrassed just watching him. *The Taurus angle*, Matthews. That's beginner shit. I could line that one up from Mars orbit."

"He'll get the hang of it. Or he'll wash out."

Franks snorted. "I know which way that one'll go."

"We were all green like that too, you know. Like you didn't say the same things about me when I first came up."

Franks stared at Matthews for a long time, not saying anything, his eyes getting that distant faraway look that made Matthews uncomfortable.

"I bet you said the same things about me," he repeated

Franks blinked hard once and looked away from the table. "They're nuts if they think they're gonna replace us with them."

<BEEP>

The tone made Matthews jump. *"One. Two. Three. Four. Five,"* he counted. It had taken the machine forever to start.

The passengers were all safely in stasis when Matthews reached the angles. They had had their view of Jupiter, dominating the space to port. Now it was time to for them sleep until they got through to the other end.

Matthews tilted the ship downwards and twisted the tail back towards the sun so he faced the angles. His display lit up with dozens of little yellow targets, dancing all over the glass as he manoeuvred. He was only a few hundred kilometres away now. The data points next to his target fluctuated as he eased the ship around, but he didn't look at them. Only rookies used the computer.

Matthews closed his eyes…and there it was. The angle. He nudged the ship around. Twist to Jupiter, pull the tail up. Shuffle sunward fifteen meters, up three. Nose down half a degree. Rotate five. *Almost there.* Shuffle up half a meter. Rotate minus two. *There, that's close.* Tilt down one degree. He could feel it. *Yes*, he had it now. He was lined up perfectly.

He pushed hard on both joysticks and the ship shot forward.

And he was through.

Everything vibrated. There was a hum. He matched the tone of it with his quivering lips because that helped. He opened his eyes slowly, so they could adjust to the bright orange glare of the sinewy in-between space.

Tendons. Threads. Infinite lines. No pattern or semblance of order. All directions at once. Points of light shot past him, around him, through him. The sturdy metal of the ship and his body rippled like water. But Matthews kept focused.

The in-between space—it did everything it could to throw you. It flashed bright in your eyes, made you numb all over. His left foot felt like it had floated away. But Matthews kept focused. The ship expanded and contracted with his breathing. He glanced down at his hands, holding firmly on to the joysticks.

There they were, right there. He could see them. Yet they also stretched out forever in front of him. His body sank through the hard wall behind him.

But Matthews kept FOCUSED.

He didn't lose himself. He kept his mind on the task. He pushed on. There was a way out of this up ahead. Or far behind. Or off to the side. It was hard to tell. Directions didn't work exactly the way they were supposed to in here. But there was an exit, somewhere. Matthews moved towards it, tugging and pulling on the joysticks to keep the ship on the right path, even as his brain stopped registering what he saw. His neck jerked convulsively, his body went rigid, and still he kept his focus. Matthews stayed on the path.

And then he was out. As if he had always been where he was.

Matthews' body went limp. His head sagged as he caught his breath, let go of the joysticks and wiped the beads of sweat from his brow. The distant stars against the black void had returned outside the cockpit. Off to starboard was the green chlorine gas giant of the Mu Arae system, over fifty light years from where they had been only moments before.

"Testing concluded. You may exit the booth. Thank you and have a nice day."

Matthews stepped out into the narrow hallway. He stared at his feet to avoid meeting the gaze of any of the techs and administrators he passed. After a few turns he felt more relaxed, as it would be less obvious to others where it was he was coming from.

It was the middle of the day (station time) on the promenade, and the area was alive and throbbing around him. People rushed about from one distraction to the next as they waited for their flights, either back down to Earth or out into the galaxy. The kiosks and small shop fronts flashed their wares at passers-by, vying for their attention.

Matthews straightened his uniform jacket and walked tall, the crowds parting for him deferentially. Most people tried not to stare as he passed, at least not so much that it would draw attention to themselves. He smiled politely, nodding at the occasional person with whom he made eye contact, knowing they were likely looking after him as he passed. Everyone wanted to be a pilot.

Earth shone brightly a few hundred miles below the observation lounge's glass window. Matthews looked down on the thick clouds obscuring the western coast of Libya. His eyes moved across the globe as the clouds cleared around the canal, until there were little more than wisps of white over the dry lands of the Middle East all the way to the horizon. Bulging over the arc of the Earth the moon was rising, half tinted blue in the ozone. He rubbed small circles with his thumbs on the polished wood of the railing as he stared at the planet.

He heard a sniffle to his left and turned to look. A pair of small dark eyes peeked out at him from the side of a soft chair where the rest of the girl was hiding. They were very intense for such a small child, he thought.

Matthews stuck his tongue out at her. Her head bobbed as she giggled. She got up slowly from her hiding spot and walked over, hugging a toy robot to her chest.

"Hello," Matthews said. The little girl didn't say anything. He continued, motioning out towards Earth. "Isn't the view pretty?"

The child glanced out the window and back at him nodding.

"Is this your first time in space?" The little girl shook her head. "You've been up here before? How many times?"

"Lots." She said shyly.

Matthews smirked. "Me too."

"'Cause you're a pilot."

"I am?"

She nodded her head furiously and pointed at him. "You're wearing your uniform."

Matthews looked down at himself in mock surprise. "Is that what this is?"

She furrowed her brow at him. "Yes. You're a pilot. I know."

Matthews smiled. "You got me. I'm a pilot."

A middle-aged man came up behind the girl. "Janelle," he said to her. "What are you doing?"

Janelle pointed at Matthews. "He's a pilot."

The man rested a hand on his daughter's shoulder and looked up at Matthews. "I'm sorry if she's bothering you, sir."

Matthews waved his apology off. "She's fine." He looked back down at the girl. "It's very nice to meet you, Janelle."

"What do you say, sweetie?" The man asked.

"It's nice to meet you," Janelle said, nibbling on her finger.

"That's my girl. We need to go find Mommy. Say goodbye to the nice man."

Janelle smiled at Matthews and waved.

The man turned to Matthews. "It was nice meeting you, sir." Matthews nodded at him as he took his daughter and turned to walk away.

After a few steps, Janelle turned back to him. "I'm gonna be a pilot too." She said solemnly.

Matthews smiled at her. "I'll save your seat."

Janelle smiled back and turned around. Matthews watched her father as they walked away. He leaned down and quietly said something to the girl, then glanced back at Matthews sheepishly, as if worried he had been overheard. The pair exited the lounge and went back out onto the promenade.

Matthews turned back to the view. He had recognised the look on Janelle's father's face when he'd whispered to his daughter. Patronising but slightly nervous, believing she'd grow out of it, move on to something else. A real life. Something safer. And she probably would. Most people gave up on their childish dreams when they grew up. But not all. The pull of it was too much for some, like it had been for him.

If she persisted, then her parents would grow truly concerned. They would tell her how hard it was to become a pilot. And about the damage it did to you even if you made it. How it could lead you in just a few short years to a lonely life of nothing, standing by yourself in a half-empty observation deck, having finished taking a cognitive test that you were absolutely sure you'd just failed.

Franks stood in the corner of the bar, staring absently at the wall, the drink in his hand about to drop at any moment. He hadn't moved a muscle since Matthews started making his way across the crowded room.

"Franks," Matthews said as he reached him. "Franks, you okay?"

The man didn't move or register that Matthews had spoken.

"Come on, snap out of it," Matthews said.

He gently put his hand on Franks' arm, planning to lead him to an empty seat nearby. But as he touched him, Franks blinked hard and looked at Matthews. "What?"

"Are you alright?" Matthews asked. "Had a little too much to drink, maybe?"

Franks glanced around the room, a slight look of panic in his eyes. Everyone avoided looking at him, pretending he wasn't there. He took a deep drink and turned back to Matthews. "It's nothing. I'm fine. When did you get in?"

"Just a few minutes ago."

Franks smiled at him. "Well it's about time. Damn boring in here tonight. Come on, let's hit that new place on the third level."

Matthews nodded and let Franks, back to his old self, lead him away as if nothing had happened. Which was fine with Matthews. He didn't want to think about it either.

It wasn't just a lack of focus; that alone wouldn't flunk a pilot. Most pilots were pretty flaky to begin with. It was the periods of absence, when a pilot could have sworn they were somewhere else, some *when* else—earlier, even later. Meanwhile in everyone else's world you were frozen in place like a statue. Or you had moments where you seemed to exist at a different speed than the rest of the world, far too fast or slow. The simple thirty-minute test could take up to three hours to get through if you were in really bad shape.

That's what the angles did to you. They messed with time. The more you flew the angles, the more you drifted away from linear existence. The test looked for long pauses while counting or counting at an erratic pace. Or just the far away comportment washing over you as you counted, when it was clear you were someplace else. If the test picked up too much of that, you were as good as grounded.

Weiters sighed and leaned forward on his desk. "How many years have you been a pilot, Matthews?"

"It'll be fourteen in a couple of months."

"Which is almost three times longer than Jacobs—twice as long as Suarez or Mindoye. Hell, that's four more than any pilot I've ever heard of."

"Franks made it twelve," Matthews said.

"Right. Franks." Weiters continued. "What could you possibly have to prove to anyone anymore?"

Matthews didn't say anything, watching the dust in the lamplight dance.

"You have a great pension, plus whatever you've saved up all these years. All that makes for a pretty damn comfortable life. And you're still young so you can really enjoy it too. The damage isn't bad yet. Just a little drifting. No big deal."

"Then why am I being grounded?"

Weiters pounded his fist on the desk. "Because it's the law. I have to. You know that." He sat back in his chair breathing deeply. "Look. I can hold off on entering the results and you can just retire quietly. Tell everyone you just thought it was time. Or you met someone and want to settle down and relax. Whatever you want. Nobody has to know."

A large mote of dust fell straight down into the light.

Matthews sat by himself in the pilot lounge, just off the locker rooms and staging area. It was a small room, all grey, with modest decor on the sloping walls that seemed to flow into the glass and brass of the bar in the far corner. Rectangular viewports ran across the outer wall at eye level, and tables were scattered haphazardly around the room, with a pair of plush soft chairs each. There was no blaring music or the hum of humanity that you couldn't escape from on the promenade, just the soft hiss of the station's air scrubbers filtering in through the vents. It was a relaxing place to hang out in without the staring crowds, and many pilots liked to take advantage of it for the privacy.

Apart from Matthews and the bartender Sid, there were only a couple of green pilots sitting on the other side of the room. Matthews glanced at them. A nervous little gnat—Shelby he thought her name was—was wiggling her fingers on the table as she leaned in close to talk to a pudgy kid Matthews didn't recognise. Her eyes darted over at Matthews as she finished what she was saying and sipped her drink. The other kid turned his head and glanced back at him. Their eyes met for just a moment before he looked away quickly back to Shelby, who was doing everything she could not to look in Matthews' direction.

"Franks," Matthews said insistently, pushing him gently on the arm.

Franks grimaced and looked over at Matthews, annoyed. "I was just thinking dammit. I didn't go anywhere." He flicked his empty shot glass down the bar with his finger.

Matthews shook his head. "When is it official?"

"As of two hours ago," Franks replied. "I'm done."

"You can fight it. You should fight it."

"How?"

Matthews looked around the room. "Hell, I don't know. Tell them you were hungover and take the test again."

Franks looked over at Matthews shaking his head. "Right. 'It wasn't me, chief, it was all the whiskey shots before I went in.' I don't think that'd work." Franks stared down at his hands. "Besides, I'd just fail again anyway."

"You don't know that."

"Do you think I don't notice how people look at me? Or how other pilots won't look at me at all if they can avoid it? I've been fucked up for a while now. This isn't a surprise to anyone."

"Come on, Franks—"

"Don't." He said sharply. "Just…there's no point in pretending anymore."

Matthews looked away, out of the bar window…the patchwork bright lights of the night-time Earth outlined the Eastern coast of Asia. The focal hub of Seoul was easily discernible.

"So, what will you do?" he asked Franks.

Franks shrugged. "Find a nice beach house somewhere that's always warm. Live in total comfort. Get fat and lazy. Invent new cocktails."

"Sounds horrible," Matthews said.

"Yeah." Franks laughed. "At least with my mushed-up brain I won't spend all my time there."

Matthews tried to laugh with him. But the dread in his bones was just too much to do it convincingly.

The door across the room to the staging area slid open, and Shera, the embarkment chief stepped through. She walked straight to the bar and leaned heavily on top of it, rubbing her face then sticking a few errant dreads behind her ear. Sid approached with a sandwich and placed it down in front of her.

Matthews got up from his table and made his way over to Shera. "Rough day?" he said as he leaned next to her on the bar.

Shera looked up from her food, shaking her head as she swallowed. "Oh, you have no idea. Been one headache after another all shift. I got three cockpits down with inspection fails, a ship all ready to go out to Mu Arae without a pilot because Guilfoye broke his thrusters getting back here from Seti, so he arrived a day late and threw all the schedules off, and the new techs they stuck me with couldn't find their own ass with a flashlight and help from a supervisor."

"So about normal." Matthews said.

Shera slapped him lightly on the shoulder. "I swear I'm gonna quit."

Matthews laughed. "It'll never happen. You love this and you know it." Shera shrugged and took another bite of her lunch.

Matthews looked around the room for a moment as Shera ate. "What was that you said about a ship without a pilot?"

Matthews let the ship drift aimlessly in space, tumbling slowly over itself. He had turned off the lights and muted all the sounds in the cockpit. The only light came from the green glow of the gas giant out to port. Normally he would have already set his course and moved inwards, towards the distant star at the centre of the system where the colonies were, but he wanted to just drift and relax for a moment. The passengers were still in stasis, and the system entry base was on the other side of the gas giant. There was no one to care.

Outside was so peaceful, so constant and unchanging. The clouds of the massive ball of gas, even in all its chaos, seemed to be almost frozen in place, the clouds moving so slowly as to be on the very edge of perception. Lightning strikes bigger than his ship flashed here and there on the surface of the globe, but at this distance they were little more than brief sparkles or thread-thin lines, pulsing briefly then fading away.

After a while he saw the small circle of drone escorts approaching him, five white objects in a tight circle. A communication window appeared on the dome.

"Transport NEP-5968, this is Mu Arae System base, please respond." A soft voice said in his ear. Matthews said nothing. "Transport NEP-5968, this is Mu Arae System base, please respond. Are you there, Matthews?"

He sighed. "I'm here."

"Special order from Sol command. You are to follow the drone escort to System base, where a stellar pilot is to relieve you and transport the passengers on to Mu Arae prime. Confirm."

Matthews shook his head. They weren't going to let him finish the trip. Though he was surprised he had gotten this far. He wondered if Weiters had tried to cover for him when he found out Matthews had taken a ship, and got caught himself.

"Confirm." The voice said again, more forcefully. The drones were almost on top of him now. He turned on the lights and power in the cockpit and stabilised the ship to face them.

"Matthews, do you hear me? Please respond."

Matthews leaned heavily on his elbows at his desk, facing the young man in the white scrubs on the laptop screen. His body felt a thousand times heavier than it had a moment ago.

"I'm sorry sir, but Mr. Franks isn't able to accept any calls," the man said, somewhat coldly. "He is not having one of his good days. You could try again tomorrow, but I can't promise he would be much better. I can let him know you called when he comes back to us if you like. But it might be some time."

Matthews hit the thrusters. The sudden g-force pressed him against the wall so hard his vision went red, and he blew right past the escorts. Beyond the throbbing in his ears he could vaguely hear the voice from system base, now yelling at the top of its lungs at him.

The dive into the planet had confused the drones and gained him some distance. But he could already see them off to his side catching up. One shot from their EM pulse guns and his engines would shut down permanently.

He turned off the main engines and reached for the lever by his left leg, pulling the joystick in his right hand as far to the side as he could. The ship went into a tight spin with its centre of mass just behind the cockpit. The gas giant flew past and came back around in just a few seconds. Then in less than one. The spinning picked up speed. His ribs pressed hard into the armrest, shooting pain up his side. But he kept going. Faster. His harness started to choke him as the centrifugal force tried to throw him outward. The world outside the cockpit became a quickly alternating blur of black and green. He fought the urge to be sick. Or pass out. He had to time this just right...

NOW.

He pulled the lever. There was a loud clank and the whine of bending metal as the cockpit broke free, sending the passenger compartments hurling back towards the drones.

By the time he stabilised himself, facing backward, the compartments were already several dozen kilometres away, still spinning wildly. He could see no structural damage apart from where he had ripped free of the connecting lines, and the drones' programming had kicked in, prioritising saving the passengers over chasing him.

"Transport NEP-5968, this is Station Commander Levisson." A stern voice blared in his ear. "What in the fucking hell do you think you're doing? You will power down this instant and wait for retrieval. That is a direct order. I will authorise lethal force—"

Matthews shut off the communication as he spun the cockpit around. The main engines had gone with the compartments, but he still had the docking thrusters. He had also lost a good deal of speed during his stunt, and eventually one of the drones would break off and go after him.

He dived towards the planet. If he could slingshot around it, he could gain all the speed he needed. And with one strong burst from all the thrusters at the right moment, he could shoot back out towards the angles and the drones would never catch him. And then he could go anywhere.

The gas giant grew large in front of him. The planet lost its flat appearance and he saw the rough, uneven clouds as they flowed through each other. A shaft of lightning stretched out like a river below, all the way around the bend of the planet.

He fell farther, his speed increasing rapidly. The cockpit shook and groaned violently as its outer dome began to glow. He started to list to the right, the ship pointing down towards the planet. His angle had been too steep—he was falling too fast. He fired the thrusters to try and gain some altitude, hoping he would still have enough left to gain escape velocity afterwards.

But nothing happened. He tried again and still nothing. Something was wrong. The manoeuvring thrusters were only working at half power, not enough to counteract the pull of the gas giant. They must have been damaged in the separation. Without them, he had no way of breaking free, no way to stop from plunging down into the clouds below to be crushed.

The shaking increased, and Matthews gritted his teeth. His head bounced against the wall. He gripped the joysticks so hard his shoulders felt like they were about to shatter. He saw tiny fractures starting to spread at the seams of the glass dome as the cockpit brushed against the uppermost layer of clouds, the green chaos swirling like a nightmare, opening to swallow him whole.

Matthews closed his eyes. It hadn't been much of an idea in the first place. Where could he have gone anyway that they wouldn't be able to find him?

Then he felt it up ahead of him. There was an angle.

He opened his eyes and looked down at the planet. He was on the edge of a giant vortex in the centre of a dark cloud, lightning continuously rippling down its sides. Down there, that's where he had felt the angle, in that monster. But it was impossible. Angles didn't form in planets. There were no opposing gravities to form one. The pull of that storm against itself couldn't possibly be enough.

But he could feel it, far, far down in the vortex. It was there. Yet out of reach. The pressure and the turbulence would likely rip him to pieces before he could reach it. But if he could…

"Might as well try it," Franks said. "Not like you got anything to lose."

Matthews closed his eyes again, stopped fighting against the pull of the giant, and plunged straight down. The cockpit immediately started come apart, cracking and splitting, fuses blowing around him. His head was being crushed from all sides at once. But he blocked it out. *Nudge a little to the left. There, fine. Just fine.* He heard the cracks in the dome getting larger, and then a deafening roar and a gush of air away from him as it finally broke open. His body was yanked forwards but the straps of his harness prevented him from getting sucked out. His throat burned as he caught a whiff of the planet's atmosphere. He held his breath, didn't open his eyes or shout. He needed to concentrate. Still on target, he could feel it lined up. Blood trickled down his cheeks from his nose, his ears, his closed eyelids, and froze against his skin. His entire body screamed at him. But he was almost there. He could sense it. It was lined up perfectly.

And he was through.

"NEP-5968, this is Mu Arae System Base. Please respond."

"Repeat. NEP-5968, this is Mu Arae System Base. Please respond. Matthews, are you there?"

Levisson leaned over the communications officer, staring intently at the planet. "Answer me!" He shouted. But there was no reply.

He stood up, sighing heavily and rubbing his neck. "Shut it down, Tara."

"Yes, sir." Tara closed the communications window on the overhead and brought the system traffic monitor back up. She turned in her seat to face the commander. "What do you want me to tell Sol control?"

"Tell them that Matthews was lost when his cockpit malfunctioned. There was nothing we could do to save him. He managed to jettison his compartments clear of danger before he spun into the marble."

"Sir? What about the arrest order?"

Levisson shook his head. "I'm sure you're going to find that that order was rescinded. Or will be. Just a glitch in the system." Levisson turned away from her. "Just give the broad brushstrokes to them for now. It was equipment failure. I'll file the formal report in the morning."

Levisson exited the bridge for his executive quarters, leaving the bridge crew to their work.

A very thin dark line ran along the equator of the gas giant, as if something had screamed across the grain. It was already dissipating into nothing.

The Blargulon 7 Information Kiosk

Featured in Issue #77

…Rose West

You *have chosen: English*
Welcome, visitor!
You have chosen: Human
Welcome, climate refugee!
Choose an option
You have chosen: Nutritional Establishments in the Local Geographic Area
There are two nutritional establishments suitable for humans within reasonable human walking distance:
The Blargulon Park Portable Eatery
Florflorax's Human Meat Emporium (note: translation may be inaccurate).
You have chosen the Blargulon Park Portable Eatery. This establishment has three different foodstuffs that have been deemed safe for human consumption and nutritious to the human body.

The skitterax on a stick is a small, six-legged creature similar to the extinct Earth porcupine. It is lightly heated and served on a stick so that its glandular sac remains intact; the juices contained in this sac are high in vitamins B and E. Skitterax on a stick is a regional delicacy; be sure to burst the sac with your tongue for the authentic skitterax experience.

The schlumplette is a dish composed of chopped scrofula roots and lingus eggs; this may be appropriate for human vegetarians who consider eggs a vegetable (note: translation may be inaccurate).

Zzzzizt is a lukewarm slab of zim protein with a brown sauce. It is considered to be similar to human "tofu," which is now also extinct due to your reckless mismanagement of the Earth's natural resources (note: translation may be inaccurate).
Exit
Choose an option
You have chosen: Communal Evacuation Stations
There are six communal evacuation stations in Blargulon Park. Their locations appear in blue on the diagram below.

You have chosen the Blargulon Memorial Evacuation Station. This station is approved for human use; there is a separate entrance clearly marked with the human symbol on the left-hand side of the building as you go in the main entrance.

Please note that until Blargulon City is able to upgrade its facilities to cope with the large influx of refugees, all humans will be required to use the communal Blargulon-style evacuation stations.

If you require an evacuation station that services only one gender, see options for Blargulon Veterans' Square, located 15 kilometres to the east of your current location.

If you require a private evacuation station, please see options for the Planet Earth Embassy on Squintax Avenue. However, as a new arrival on Blargulon 7, it would be an invaluable experience for you to show your gratitude by joining your fellow beings in the joyful expression of a communal evacuation.

Exit

Choose an option

You have chosen: Conveyances

Choose a destination

You have chosen: Planet Earth Embassy

The most common form of conveyance to the interplanetary neighbourhood of Squintax is the velocipod. Most humans find these uncomfortable, as the size and shape is incorrect for your humanoid form; however, velocipods are a cheap and easy way to explore your new neighbourhood—and maybe to get up close and personal with some of your neighbours as you mingle in the stomach of the velocipod! It is very likely that after you have taken your first few rides and adjusted your bodily chemicals accordingly, you will be taking various types of public conveyances just as easily as a native Blarguloner.

Exit

Choose an option

You have chosen: Hydration Sources

The nearest chronological entertainment event in Blargulon Memorial Park is the biannual Sharing of the Fluids. The nearest geographical hydration source to this information kiosk is the Flemulon Canal. If you look around the park, you will see many of these lovely canals full of interesting-looking liquids (note: translation may not be accurate). These canals can be used for hydration, although only if you are accompanied by a Blarguloner with whom you intend to share your bodily fluids in a private ceremony.

You may also wish to participate in the official ceremony, which is a beloved Blargulon tradition. Join your new neighbours as they feast on the moist canal fluids, mingling neighbour with neighbour in a communal experience of joy. Be sure to watch out for the moulting youths—visitors who are not aware of their surroundings are often taken unawares! If you would like to assimilate into Blargulon life, the Sharing of the Fluids is an absolute must.

Hydration sources suitable for single human use are available at the locations in purple below. Please note that there is a mandatory 1-litre limit per genetic signature per day, as climate refugees are not permanent citizens and have not yet proven their ability to respect and conserve our planet's natural resources.

Exit

Choose an option
You have chosen: Translation
You have chosen: Flemulon

Flemulon: a liquid and moist outpouring of expression being of joy from one to all (note: translation may be inaccurate).

As a new arrival on Blargulon 7, it would behove you to begin learning the Blargulon language in a show of gratitude toward your new Blarguloner hosts. Although it may be difficult for the human voice box to pronounce the sixty particular tones essential to fluency in Blargulon, making an effort will show that you are eager to abandon your simple human languages as part of the process of fully assimilating into Blargulon society.

Exit

Choose an option
You have chosen: Citizenship

Becoming a Blargulon citizen is an arduous yet rewarding process (note: translation may be inaccurate). Since you are already here enjoying the many delightful resources of Blargulon 7, you have already submitted the necessary prerequisite paperwork in order to be considered an official refugee.

As a refugee, your status is legally protected under Code 000X1-Alpha-Beta-Theta-63487, although this may be rescinded at any time. Your refugee status entitles you to no benefits aside from your subsidised government housing, for which you will owe the government retroactively when you become a citizen and obtain employment. As a refugee, it is your responsibility to obtain employment.

After having lived and worked on Blargulon 7 for a minimum of two solar cycles (excluding the Wet Season) but not more than five solar cycles (including the Ultra-Moist Season), you will be expected to show your knowledge of and interest in Blargulon history and civilisation by passing a series of citizenship tests, including but not limited to history, culture, language proficiency (in which you must demonstrate a minimum level of knowledge equivalent to Theta-65), monetary usefulness, labour motivation, and Flemulon participation.

Should you pass these citizenship tests (note: translation may not be accurate), your status will be upgraded to "Citizen in Transition," under which you have no legal protections but will be expected to maintain a minimum level of Blargulax moistness. At this time, it is also recommended that you progress to the Theta-200 level of Blargulon language proficiency, which requires a minimum of forty-five thorax-generated aural frequencies.

Enjoy this time on Blargulon 7! After only several more solar cycles (not including the Semi-Moist Season), you will be legally authorised to begin to attempt the final round of citizenship tests, assuming you have maintained consistent employment with no gaps and lived at the same location or abode for your entire stay on the planet. If—

Exit

Goodbye

ANDROMEDA SPACEWAYS

Magazine

Subscriptions

Make sure you get the latest issue of *Andromeda Spaceways Magazine* as soon as it comes out.

Buy a First Class Subscription ticket and get brand-new fiction for just $18 per year—in EPUB, MOBI or PDF formats. We'll also throw in some members-only goodies for you to enjoy.

Make your way to www.andromedaspaceways.com/subscribe to get your subscription.

All enquiries can be made to accounts@andromedaspaceways.com

The Photographs

Featured in Issue #75

...Michael Gardner

"**L**unch is ready," Cal yelled, as he placed a plate of sandwiches on the cast iron table on the weathered deck.

"Shouldn't you be helping him?" Missy asked. She put three beers on the table next to the sandwiches.

"Probably."

Cal stepped off of the edge of the deck and dropped to his haunches so he could peer under the house. His brother, Tom, was commando crawling towards him, covered in sweat and dust and swearing under his breath. In his left hand, a Stillson pipe wrench; in his right, an old wooden box about a foot wide and long.

"Give me a hand, will ya?" Tom said, as he held out the wrench. Cal took it and placed it on the deck. Then he offered Tom his hand and helped pull him out from under the house.

"What's this?" Cal asked, as Tom handed him the box and then began to dust down the front of his clothes.

"No idea, but it's bloody solid. It was wedged up under your house near the pipes. I didn't know it was there until I knocked it loose. The damn thing smacked me on the melon. I'm lucky I'm not concussed."

Cal turned the box in his hands. It was heavy. There were no markings or decoration that he could see, although there was a fine seam around the top, which suggested a lid. But he couldn't see any obvious latch or handle.

"Can I have a look?" Missy asked. Cal shrugged and handed it to her. "There's something in it," she said as she held it up to her ear and shook it gently. She began to trace her fingernails around the seam.

Cal heard a click and saw that Missy had pried loose a small rectangle of wood about an inch long. It flipped out on a hidden hinge. She pushed her little finger into the gap, and there was a second click. Then the top of the box popped open, dislodging dust. Missy turned and placed the box on the table, pulling the lid open before she sat down. Tom and Cal stepped up onto the deck and joined her at the table, Tom grabbing a beer and taking a swig.

"What's in it?" Tom asked after he'd swallowed loudly.

"Photographs," Missy replied, reaching in. "This one's of our house, isn't it?" She handed Cal an eight by ten black and white photo, yellowed with age.

"Yeah, it looks like the house," he said. The paint was fresh, the old brick chimney was in one piece, and the house was surrounded by low cut stumps where the land had just been cleared. A bright light burned through the front window, Cal noticed. He flipped the photo over. Written on the back in pencil was "1908," nothing else. He placed the photo in front of Tom.

Missy passed Cal a second photo. Another picture of the house, but from the back.

Next, a photo of a woman standing on the deck. Her hair was parted straight down the middle and pulled back tight over her ears. She had a long, slender nose and beady eyes. A bright light blazed through the frosted window over her left shoulder. Cal paused, his eyes drawn to that light. It was the same crescent shape as in the first photo. And it shone through the same window. He passed the photo to Tom.

Then, another photo of the same woman sitting in a rocking chair in the main bedroom, holding a baby.

The next was a family photo. The beady eyed lady stood between a tall, wiry man with dark hair, and a dark-haired boy of about five. They all stared straight down the camera, and at Cal from the distant past. Again, a fiery crescent glowed behind the frosted window just behind the family. What was that? Cal wondered. *A fault in the photographs? Something else?*

Cal passed the photo to Tom.

"That light's odd, isn't it?" Tom said, as if reading Cal's mind.

"Yeah," Missy responded. "It can't be a fire, there's no fireplace in the lounge room."

"It might be overexposure," Cal suggested.

"In the same spot in each photo?" Tom replied.

"Well what do you think it is?"

"I don't know, but—"

"Whoa," Missy interrupted them. "Look at this and tell me if you still think it's overexposure."

Missy held out a Polaroid, which Cal accepted.

The photo was of revellers at a party. It had been taken from the hallway of the house, looking into the lounge room where the red, floral carpet looked almost new. Closest to camera was a petite blonde with curly hair, waving. Just behind her and to the right was an attractive Aboriginal man with a broad smile. And next to him, floating about waist high, was something Cal at first mistook as fire—a slender crescent shape, bright red and orange at the edges, but black in the middle, like the air glowed red hot where someone had roughly torn it apart to expose a nothingness beyond. The skin on Cal's neck crawled. It's wrong, plain wrong, he thought. He had the urge to tear the photo up and throw it to the wind, and yet he didn't. He held onto it grimly, staring.

"That's not a fault in the photo," Missy said. Cal grunted non-committedly.

He turned the photo over and took a deep breath to still the quaver in his fingers. A message, scrawled in pen, filled the back of the photo:

We took this the night David died. We didn't notice the light at the time. Was it there when the photo developed? Did it come later? It's a bit like the other photos, the old ones we showed David only the week before. What had he said again? Something like: 'My people believed that everything is connected—the past, present and future, the living and dead, the spirit world and this one, and all of it tied to the land. My ancestors once roamed these hills, and camped where your house stands today. To me, it looks like one of their campfires, from long ago, is still burning.'

RIP, David Jurrah, 1985.

"Cal," Missy said.

Cal, startled, dropped the photo and looked up. She was holding a video cassette with masking tape affixed to the side. Whatever had been written on it had faded, no longer legible.

"They must have put all of this in the box for a reason," she said, her eyes sparkling, enjoying the moment.

Cal stared at Missy, then the video, and as he did something heavy settled in his stomach. Whatever was on that tape, he didn't want to see it. The photos were weird enough. Yet, if he voiced his concerns, it would sound irrational and superstitious.

"Jesus," Tom said. He'd picked up the Polaroid from the table and was looking at it, wide eyed.

"Hey, what's written on the back?" Missy asked.

Tom flipped it over and read it to himself. "Geez, that's creepy," he said, before handing the photo to Missy.

As Missy read the back of the photo, her eyes moistened. Finally, when finished, she placed it carefully on the table.

"I don't think it's creepy," she said, looking at Tom, and then Cal. "I think it's beautiful. What a wonderful idea, that everything is connected. That different places in this world have links to the past, the future, and those… that have left us behind."

She cleared her throat. Cal knew she was thinking of her Dad. He watched her turn the photo over and look at the image again. Then she looked at the window behind her.

"It's probably a hoax," Cal said more sharply than he'd intended.

Missy turned back and looked at him quizzically. Cal averted his eyes and picked up a sandwich, munching methodically, like a cow chewing cud. Missy started gathering up the photos and returning them to the wooden container.

"Do you have a VCR, Tom?" Missy asked as she picked up the tape. Cal stopped chewing.

"Sorry, Miss. Haven't had one for years. But Allie might. The library loans out DVDs, so they must have had videos once. Maybe they still have an old machine out back." Tom looked at his watch. "The library's open till three. If you left now you'd catch her, I reckon."

"What do you think, Cal? Can you do without me for the afternoon?"

What could he say? Could he ban her from investigating this further based on an irrational fear of what might end up just being a blank tape? Cal swallowed his mouthful and forced himself to smile.

"Sure, honey."

Cal pushed open the front door and found Missy sitting on the floor in front of the TV, a pile of books on her left; an old, scratched VCR on her right. Cal frowned.

"Hi, honey," Missy said cheerily. "Can you give me a hand?

He sighed, then shuffled into the room. *It's just a video,* he thought.

"So, you found one," he said, trying to sound casual, afraid he'd failed abysmally.

"Yeah, the library didn't have one, but Allie directed me to this little store that fixes appliances. The owner was closing when I showed up, but when I told him what I was after, he was nice enough to open the shop back up. They had a few second-hand VCRs for sale. This beauty only cost me fifteen dollars."

"Hmm," Cal said as he knelt. He plugged the power cord and AV cables into the VCR.

"Allie also helped me to find a heap of information about the house and this area. Did you know part of the Kamilaroi tribe use to live around here? She gave me a few books about them."

Cal ran the cables up over the TV cabinet and into the TV.

"There you go. Can't guarantee it will work, but it's plugged in," he said as he sat on the floor.

"Yay," Missy said, clapping her hands together. "You ready?"

Cal hesitated, nodded.

Missy withdrew the video cassette from the wooden box on the cabinet and placed it in the machine. She turned on the TV and pressed play, then sat down next to Cal.

The VCR *whirred*, two white lines vibrating across the screen, then the machine stopped with a *clunk*. Missy pressed play again, but nothing happened. She tried to eject but got the same result.

"Well, that was a waste of fifteen bucks," she said, as she banged the top of the VCR with the flat of her hand.

"Oh well," Cal said, relieved, "you tried."

"I'll just take it back first thing Monday and see if they can fix it," she said.

Cal swallowed, then forced a grin.

"Sure, honey," he said as his heart beat hard, heat rising in his neck and cheeks.

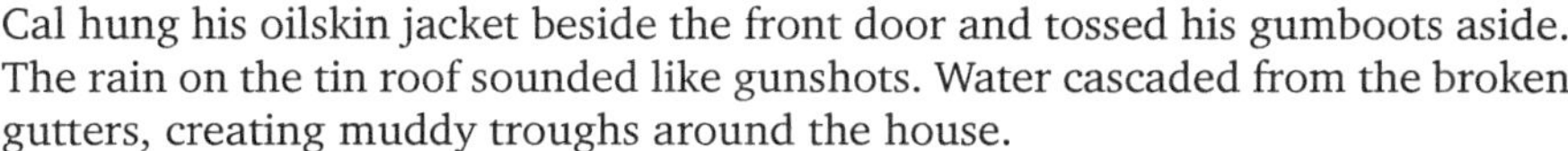

Cal hung his oilskin jacket beside the front door and tossed his gumboots aside. The rain on the tin roof sounded like gunshots. Water cascaded from the broken gutters, creating muddy troughs around the house.

Cal walked into the lounge room in his socks, running his hands back and forth through his wet hair. He heard Missy singing along to the radio in the kitchen. The scent of a tomato sauce permeated the house. His mouth watered.

As he moved towards the hall, he noticed that the wooden box sat on their coffee table, along with some of the photos and an open library book. He changed direction and approached the book. Attached to the open pages were several newspaper cut-outs of obituaries from 1910. A red ribbon jutted out of the back of the book, which he presumed Missy must have used to mark a page.

Cal picked up one of the photos next to the book—the family photo of the stern man, his serious wife, and their young boy—and placed it between the open pages. Then he flipped the book open to the ribbon. An identical photo stared back at him—the only difference being that the boy was missing. *Maybe it had been taken on the same day*, he thought, attempting to convince himself otherwise.

Written under the photo: *Mr and Mrs Donald Ramsey of "Lockleed," 1914.* The accompanying article talked about a ram that they had bred, which won grand champion at the show the reporter apparently had covered.

Cal replaced the ribbon and flipped through the rest of the book. Each page contained newspaper articles. He flipped it closed. Written on the front cover in a neat hand was: *Articles from the Gunnedah Advertiser, 1908 to 1916.*

It's a fancy scrap book really, Cal mused.

He opened the book again, returning to the obituaries. He removed the family photo he'd used as a book mark and saw it straight away.

The hair prickled on the back of his neck. The second entry on the left page read: *Mr and Mrs Donald Ramsey and family and friends mourn the sad passing of their only son, William Ramsey, who passed away unexpectedly in his cot. 5 May 1909 to 7 June 1910. A funeral will be held this Thursday, 9 June 1910.*

They must have had another son. Cal stared at the family photo lying on the coffee table then slammed the book shut.

He began to rise when he spied another of Missy's library books on the couch—"Aboriginal ghost stories." He picked it up and browsed. There was a page on bunyips and one on willy willies. One on cannibals, vampire-like beings, and even something that resembled a mermaid. Then he discovered a two-page spread. On the left, a crude ochre painting of a woman with horns on her shoulders. On the right, a similar style picture of a being with huge genitalia. *Kurriwilban*, the text underneath the first painting read, *was a demon with horns on her shoulders that she used to impale young men. Her cannibalistic husband, Koyorowen, killed and roasted women.* Cal snapped the book shut and dropped it on the couch with an unsteady hand. *I'll feel better after a shower.*

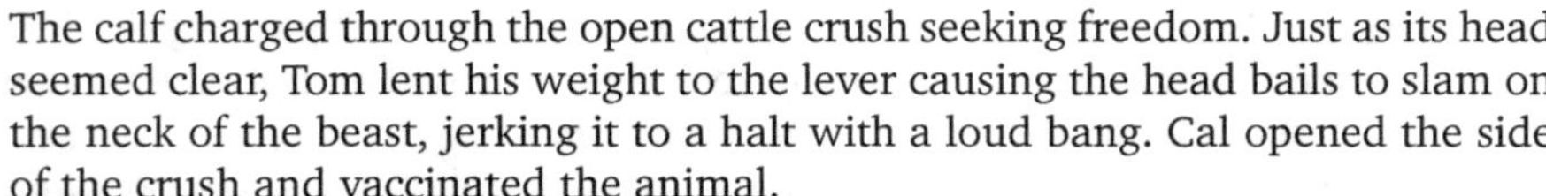

The calf charged through the open cattle crush seeking freedom. Just as its head seemed clear, Tom lent his weight to the lever causing the head bails to slam on the neck of the beast, jerking it to a halt with a loud bang. Cal opened the side of the crush and vaccinated the animal.

"Horns on this one," Tom bellowed, reaching into the bucket of disinfectant for the de-horners. Cal grabbed the brand from the fire, which glowed red hot. It momentarily brought to his mind the strange crescent in the photo of David Jurrah. He pushed the image away and seared the rump of the beast. The calf bellowed, its cry joining in with the *moo-ahs* of the rest of the stock. It bellowed even louder when Tom clamped down on the de-horners, cutting a crescent into its skull. As Tom wrenched the horn loose, a long spurt of red blood hissed through the air and arced into the dirt.

As Tom worked the de-horners onto the second horn, Cal heard the rumbling of a car above the cries of the cattle. He looked out across the yards and saw Missy pull up in her Corolla. She cut the engine and emerged wearing jeans and a black jumper. Cal waved and smiled, then ushered her toward the race.

"You coming to help us out?" Cal asked as she approached.

Missy wrinkled her nose and shook her head. "I'm not sure I'm ready for that," she said, gesturing to the bleeding calf in the crush. "I'm off to town to see Allie and see if I can get that VCR fixed."

"Oh," Cal said, "Okay. Well, I'll see you tonight."

"Will do. Bye, Tom," she yelled out.

Tom gave her a big grin and a wave. Then she blew Cal a kiss and returned to her car. Cal watched her drive away, leaving a trail of dust.

Cal hoped that the new machine would be broken like the last, but, when Missy pressed play, the VCR whirred softly, and the TV began to hiss, as black and grey static danced across the screen.

Missy joined Cal on the couch, took his hand in hers, and squeezed gently. Outside, the sun was setting, bathing the lounge room in pink light. But Cal was focussed on the TV.

Just when he thought that the tape might be blank, the screen clarified into the image of the kitchen in the house. The hissing was replaced with music—the melancholy melody of Joy Division singing *Love will tear us apart*. Cal clutched Missy's hand a little tighter.

A petite woman with red, curly hair and a cream dress with puffy sleeves, her back to the camera, stood in the kitchen. She was hunched over the bench filling vol-au-vent cases with a piping bag. Cal could hear the hum of the oven to her right.

She must have felt the presence of the camera then, for she turned around. Surprised, her cheeks coloured, she waved.

"Okay, John. That's enough of me. Get that thing out of here," she said.

"You look great, honey. Is that a new dress?"

"Go out and get the party," she said, laughing. The screen blurred as John swung the camera away from the woman and toward the door. A blurry line snaked its way from the bottom of the screen to the top, then the camera bumped from side to side as John walked from the hallway to the lounge room. The music grew louder.

The camera shot fell to the floor, then it rose again, and the blurry image became clear. John stood on the periphery of the lounge room, the camera aimed at the open front door. Outside, Cal could see four people on the deck smoking. They had drinks in hand, and three of them were laughing at what the fourth had said. Inside, closer to the camera, three people were standing in a group and yelling so that their voices wouldn't be drowned out by the music, but the video didn't pick up what they were saying. And in the corner, on a cane chair, was an old, wiry man.

"I know him," Missy said. "That's Donald Ramsey."

"No," Cal said. "This is, what, the eighties? He'd be long dead."

"But it's him. Look. Tall, wavy hair, stooped."

The camera zoomed in on the man. *It's not him*, Cal told himself. *But, then again, could it be?* The man in the video bore a striking resemblance to the photos he had seen of Donald Ramsey—the one from the box and the one in the scrap book. *This is crazy*, Cal thought. *A relative maybe. That would make more sense.*

Suddenly the camera swung to the left. Five people were dancing in the far corner of the room in front of a record player. The image bumped and jolted as John approached the group.

"Hey, Davo, you having fun?" John asked. A big, balding man turned to the camera and gave a thumbs up and a smile. A pretty, blonde woman next to him waved. The others continued to shuffle drunkenly to the music.

The camera turned again, making Cal feel queasy. When the image steadied, it had found David Jurrah. He was wearing the same floral shirt as in the Polaroid. He smiled broadly and looked dead at the camera. And just to his left, about waist high, floated the red-hot crescent framing a centre of inky blackness.

Cal's gaze was drawn to it. The red-orange edge pulsed and shimmered, like coals in a fire. But Cal focussed completely on the blackness within. There was depth there, like a window through which he could see into another world. A dark world.

The camera shot zoomed slowly as David talked, but Cal didn't really hear him. He sensed movement in the darkness. Something shifting that was perhaps a shade lighter than black. A grey-blue shadow dancing amongst the black ones. Cal squinted and concentrated harder. *Yes, something is definitely moving.*

The camera zoomed again, stopped. The grey-blue shadow was floating. It shifted, slowly, and clarified into something bipedal, two long limbs and two shorter, but all four were writhing rhythmically. It appeared to be a long way from the window, and yet, it was drawing slowly closer. Did it see this world through the crescent as Cal saw its?

Its form became clearer. Cal saw a head, distinct from the broad torso. It reached out with one shadowy limb towards the crescent, towards the camera, towards the screen. Hazy digits opened and closed, like it was trying to claw itself towards the precipice. Cal's heart thumped hard against his ribcage, like a bird smashing into a window.

The shadow shifted again, and two yellow, rheumy eyes opened in its head. It stared at the camera and pointed towards the screen. An orifice opened below the eyes, silently screaming, exposing a maw filled with red flames. Then static.

Cal was breathing shallowly, his stomach a knot. Missy clutched him tightly. Neither said anything while the video continued broadcasting grey pixelated rain, the soundtrack a dull hiss.

Cal cleared his throat. He wanted to share his horror with Missy. He wanted to talk and make sure he was still sane.

"Is that the end?" was all he managed to get out.

"I don't know," Missy replied. She twisted in the chair so that she and Cal were face-to-face. "You saw that too, right? It was... Well, I don't really know, but it felt like I was looking into some other realm."

Into something horrific, Cal thought. Into some place he couldn't explain and something he didn't want to ever see again.

"It was amazing," Missy continued.

Cal, startled, felt his mouth drop open. As he looked at her, she didn't see the dread he felt. She looked excited.

Cal cleared his throat again. "I... I don't know if we saw the same thing," he said.

Missy disentangled her hand from Cal's, then approached the VCR and began to fast forward. The machine whirred loudly. Cal and Missy watched more static dance across the screen. Then the video stopped with a *clunk*; the screen went black. Missy hit rewind and turned back to Cal. She had tears in her eyes.

"Since Dad passed," Missy began hesitantly, "I've wondered... We were never religious, but..." she took a deep breath, hugged herself. "Do you know what the Aboriginals believed in?"

"Like the Dreaming, the rainbow serpent, that sort of thing?"

"The Dreaming is a poor white term for hundreds of different belief systems. We tend to have this idea of the Dreaming being a story of creation or something, but it's more complex than that. I've been looking through the books Allie gave me. The Dreaming is both our world and the spirit world. It's all places, and it's all times co-existing, but still separate. It's the connection between the land, the people, and the spirits of their ancestors."

And demons and monsters, Cal thought, thinking back to the paintings of

Kurriwilban and Koyorowen. He swallowed.

"I like that idea," Missy said. "What if we just saw part of it? A connection wrought visible on tape?"

"You think that's what we just watched?"

"Why not? We saw a ghost sitting not far from a red framed window through which we saw another world."

An element of what she said made sense. And yet, he didn't share her optimism. A deep uneasiness gripped him.

"I didn't see any such thing. I saw an old man and a fault in the video."

"Oh, come on, Cal. A fault in the video? And the photos as well? This is something else. Don't you see? It's proof that death is not the end. It's proof that I'm not crazy when…"

"When what?"

Missy turned away from Cal.

"When I talk to Dad. And I feel like… No, I'm certain he's listening."

Cal rose on unsteady legs. He didn't see hope in that tape. He saw something terrifying. And he didn't know why she didn't feel the same.

"I know you miss your Dad," he said slowly and carefully. "And please, keep talking to him. And wherever he has gone, I hope he can hear you. But I don't believe that video will help you find him again."

Missy's eyes narrowed, then she turned from him, bent down, and hit play on the VCR. The static was back on the screen.

"What are you doing?" Cal asked, exasperated.

"Watching it again."

Cal thought of arguing but changed his mind. He turned from Missy and marched from the room.

Cal found Missy sitting on the deck in her pyjamas, playing with her phone. On the table next to her was a half empty cup of tea and a book on Indigenous Australian cultures.

Missy looked up at him with sad eyes. Cal sighed.

"I'm sorry about last night," he said. "I know the last few months have been tough for you. But I love you."

"I'm sorry too."

Cal leaned over and hugged her, breathing in her earthy, sleepy scent. He let her go and sat down next to her. He hated fighting, and yet he didn't know what to say next. He was truly sorry for upsetting her, but he remained uneasy about the video and the photos—and her views on both.

He flipped open the book on the table to a large photo of an old man waving a burning branch of eucalyptus leaves. Underneath, the caption read: *"smoking ceremonies are used to cleanse the people and ward off bad spirits."*

It was Missy that broke the silence.

"You were right," she stated. "It was probably a fault in the video. Or a hoax." Shocked, Cal looked up from the book.

"But—"

She held her phone out to him. The screen displayed a photo of their lounge room. Cal took the phone and swiped to the next photo, which was also of the lounge room. He swiped again to find the lounge room again. Then he kept swiping. Each photo was similar—the lounge room, but from slightly different angles. The lounge from the hall, the lounge from the front door, the lounge, the lounge, the lounge. All very ordinary. A ratty, run down lounge room.

"I was so convinced," Missy said. "After you went to bed I decided I'd prove it to you. So I took these photos, but none of them worked."

Cal returned the phone to her. Their fingers touched. He lingered, enjoying the warmth of her hand.

"This doesn't mean you have to stop talking to your Dad," he said.

Missy leaned over and kissed him.

When she pulled back, he said, "Why don't you come with me this morning to check on the cattle? It might be nice to show you around the farm."

"That sounds nice. But I was supposed to catch up with Allie again. I could postpone though?"

"No, don't do that. I'm happy you're getting on with her so well. Let's go for that drive tomorrow."

Missy smiled and nodded. "Okay. Well, I better get a shower so I can get going." Missy stood, kissed him on the cheek and then walked into the house.

Cal watched her leave, feeling as happy as he had for days.

"Hey, hon," Missy said when she opened the front door. She was carrying a small cardboard box under her arm. "Sorry I'm late. I lost track of time at the library, and then Allie and I grabbed a drink after. I thought you wouldn't mind."

"No, that's fine," Cal said, reaching out to Missy. She accepted his hand and allowed Cal to pull her down next to him on the couch. "But you were back at the library? I thought you were just meeting Allie for a coffee or something."

"I was," Missy said sheepishly. "It's just... I was curious about David Jurrah. I wanted to find out what happened—complete the last piece of the puzzle, you know?"

Cal cleared his throat. "Okay... So, what did you find?"

Missy placed the box on the ground and turned to Cal.

"He did die after a party here, just like it said on the back of the photo. He used to work on this property for John and Darla Kennedy—who I'm pretty sure were the camera operator and the redhead in the video. There used to be a little cottage at the bottom of this place near the road. That was David's home."

"So how did it happen?" Cal asked, recalling the image of the yellow eyed shade on the video that, now that he thought about it, could have been reaching for David Jurrah.

"It was a car accident. He lost control driving back to his cottage. The police suspected he'd been drinking, but Darla and John swore he didn't drink. There wasn't much else. There was a notice about his funeral, and I found something about Darla and John selling up about six months later. But that was it."

"Oh," Cal said. "So you're done now?"

"Yeah. I mean, I think."

"You think?"

"It's just, I was thinking again about what was written on the back of David's photo. Darla and John didn't notice the distortion until after the night it was taken. What if it appeared following David's death? And what if the white glow in the photo on the wall showed up after the Ramseys' son died? What if it is a sign from the next world? A way of communicating with those left behind? A way of saying that everything is going to be okay?" Missy lowered her gaze to her lap. "You think I'm crazy, don't you?"

Call hesitated, mulling over his response.

"Missy," he said eventually. "The other day I was reading one of your books. The one about Aboriginal ghost stories."

"And?"

Cal sucked in air. *How do I explain that the photos that gave her hope had scared the shit out of me? That I worry about her messing in stuff neither of us understand?* "What if…" Now it was his turn to look away. "What if the photos and video are, like you say, showing us something… not of this world? But what if you've misunderstood them? This land is old, Miss. Really old. And we've been here for a blink of an eye. What do we know, really? What if the things the land coughs up are best left alone?"

Missy broke out laughing and Cal felt his face redden.

"Here I was thinking you thought I was wasting my time, when actually, you're worried it's real," she said.

Cal stood quickly, his face and neck burning.

"Never mind," he snapped, before walking hastily down the hall to the bedroom

Cal woke with a start. It was dark and the room felt empty. From down the hall there came a faint *click* and then a soft *whir*. Blue light flickered through the crack left in the door, maybe from the TV.

Cal sat up. What was Missy doing? He rubbed his face, stood, and shuffled sleepily to the door. It was dark out in the hallway, but Cal could just make out the black silhouette of his wife standing at the end of the corridor, framed by the doorway to the lounge and haloed by pale blue light from the television. She raised a small box to her face, which was followed by another click and whir.

"Missy?" he rasped. The silhouette turned. She pulled something small from the box and shook it vigorously.

"Sorry, I didn't mean to wake you."

"What are you doing?" Cal asked.

"You seemed upset, so I thought I'd do this while you slept. But I had to know."

Cal took a couple of steps toward Missy as she raised the box to her face again. *Click, whir.*

"Know what?" Cal asked, trying to swallow. He kept walking.

"You know how I took the photos of the lounge room on my phone last night?"

"Yeah."

"Well, I had a thought. What if they didn't work because it was digital? What if the other photos and video worked because it was on film?"

Cal could hear the TV now. The video was playing. The party was raging, and a voice asked Davo if he was having a good time.

"What did you do?" Cal whispered, as he moved.

"I went back to that appliance store and found an old Polaroid camera."

Cal was a metre shy of Missy, when she turned and stopped him with a smile.

"It's real," she said excitedly, handing him a photo. He took it before he knew what he was doing. Suddenly his head was buzzing. And he could smell something—like the pipes in the house were backed up again. Mould and shit and something worse.

He looked at the photo. It was dull grey, but becoming clearer as it developed in the air. It was of the lounge room—lounge against the wall, frosted windows, front door. And in the middle, hovering above the old dirty carpet, was a glowing red crescent encircling blackness and a blue-grey silhouette of something long and sinewy reaching towards the camera lens. It was closer than it had been in the video. He was certain it was trying to get out.

He tore his eyes away from the photo to see that Missy had turned back to the lounge room and had raised the camera to her eye once more.

"Missy! Don't!" he screamed.

Click, whir.

When the flash from the camera lit up the lounge room, he could see it—a glowing crescent floating in the air. And reaching through it was something grey and hideous, with weeping yellow eyes and a wide mouth that screamed silently as it moved toward Missy. As quickly as it appeared, it was gone.

Cal heard the camera spit out a photo, which fluttered to the floor. He tore his eyes from the lounge room to Missy, who appeared dazed, her brow furrowed, confused. The camera slipped from her hands to clatter on the floor, and then she collapsed with a thud.

Cal rushed to her side. Her body began to spasm, slowly at first, but then harder and harder, jerking uncontrollably. Cal rolled her onto her side as she lurched back and forth, her mouth frothing red with spit and blood where she must have bitten her tongue.

"Jesus, Missy, Jesus." *Had that thing touched her? Was it still near?* he thought in a panic. He needed to get her away from here. But she was thrashing so violently that he had no choice but to hold her as best he could for the moment.

Finally, the convulsions began to slow, then she was still. His own breathing sounded ragged in his ears. He looked into the middle of the lounge room and could no longer see anything, but he could feel it—like an ice-cold breeze cooling the sweat on his forehead and neck.

He snatched up the Polaroid photos from the ground next to the broken camera and stuffed them into his pants before scooping Missy up in his arms. Then he ran out of the house and into the cool night air.

He took Missy to the edge of the lawn and placed her on the ground in front of their small shed. He patted her cheeks, trying to bring her back. Missy's eyes snapped opened and he saw her terror, her helplessness.

"Don't take me back there, don't take me back," she rambled.

"I won't, honey. We don't ever have to go back."

"Please, please," she begged, clawing weakly at his neck and shoulders, "don't take me back."

"I won't, I promise."

She grabbed his shoulders with a strength he didn't know she possessed and locked eyes with his. *I've never seen those eyes before,* he thought. They terrified him.

"Then burn it," she hissed.

Cal stared at her, shocked. *I can't do that... Can I?*

What had he seen in Missy's book only that morning? Smoke could ward off bad spirits. So what could fire do?

He didn't wait for further doubts. He left Missy on the lawn, opened the shed, and grabbed a drum of petrol. He marched into the house and began to slosh the fuel around the lounge room. The acrid scent filled the air, making Cal's eyes water. He backed out of the house, trailing fuel over the veranda, before returning the drum to the shed. He found a lighter in the glovebox of his Ute. Then he walked back to the edge of the house, hesitated for the briefest moment, flipped the lighter and tossed it.

VROOMPHHH.

The air was sucked from the world as Cal shied away, covering his face with his arm, the flames snaking across the deck and into the house, the aged wood already crackling fiercely.

"You're bloody lucky, that's all I'll tell you," Tom boomed down the phone. "I've spoken to Sergeant Robinson and he said they've decided that, technically, you haven't broken the law—provided you don't put in an insurance claim. You're not putting in a claim, are you?"

"No," Cal said quietly, as he lay on the bed in the motel room.

He hadn't been able to tell Tom the truth as to why he'd done it, even though he knew Tom had seen the photos and Allie had been helping Missy. But that wasn't the same as being there that night. Tom only knew that Missy had had some form of a breakdown, which had something to do with the house. What he thought of Cal's response, God only knew, but he wasn't talking to him the same way anymore.

"The bad news," Tom continued, "is that Ian is going to charge you seventeen hundred bucks for the call out. Your place is outside the fire brigade's jurisdiction, so they can hit you up for a fee. They'd waive it normally, he told me, but not when you set the fire yourself."

"Fair enough."

"I've given Ian details of the motel you're staying at. He'll send you an invoice in the next couple of days."

"Okay, thanks."

"Yeah, what's a brother for?" Cal could hear Tom breathing quietly on the other end of the phone. He waited. Finally, Tom spoke again, his tone softer.

"How's Missy doing? What did the Doctor say?"

"She's fine. The Doctor doesn't really know why the seizure occurred, but they're running further tests. He thinks she may have depression, so he's referred us to see a shrink."

"Hmm. Well, you look after her. I've gotta go, but we'll check in on you two tomorrow."

Cal hung up and placed his mobile on the chipped bedside table. He found the TV remote and flicked on the television. He watched the news for a while, mulling over his next move. He'd need to sell some cattle. He was flat broke, and now they needed to find somewhere to live while the farm started making money. He could probably get a decent shed built on the farm and fitted out to live in for about twenty grand. But even if it was decent, would Missy want to live back out on that land? Would he? He'd been out there twice since the fire and was convinced the fire had healed whatever thinness between the worlds had existed. He didn't feel the same unease, the same presence. Yet, could he risk it? Was it really gone?

Time to get dressed, he thought. He slid off the bed and approached his bag in the corner of the room. He sunk to his haunches and began to dig around amongst his new clothes and the loaners from Tom, when he chanced across the pants he'd worn that night. They still had the scent of smoke on them. *These definitely need a wash*.

As he pulled them from the bag, five Polaroids fell from one of the pockets and fluttered to the ground. Jesus, he thought, *I forgot about those.*

Four of the photos fell the right side up and one lay upside down. Looking at them was surreal. They showed a progression. Each displayed the same red-orange outline and darkness inside. The difference between each was the shadowy figure reaching out from its inky depths toward the camera. In the first photo, it was small and far away. The second, it had turned, its yellow eyes open. The third showed it close to the edge of the window, extending a long shadowy hand. And in the last, its mouth was an open fiery scream; its hand extended past the precipice, poised to claw at the lens of the camera.

Cal shivered.

He flipped the last photo over and saw the shadowy figure gone.

Cal stared. And stared. The blood pulsed in his temples. His chest clenched.

Was this the first photo or the last? The first or the last, he kept repeating to himself.

And then, he realised, he hadn't heard from Missy since he had phoned Tom. She'd gone to the bathroom. What was she doing?

He forced himself to his feet and approached the bathroom door.

"Missy, are you all right in there?" he asked, hoping she wouldn't hear the stammer in his voice.

There was no reply. He picked up the remote from the bed and muted the TV. "Missy?"

He leaned in close and heard soft whimpering.

"Missy?" he said again, as he gently slid the door open.

Missy was in her underwear in the empty bathtub, sobbing. Long bloody gouges marred her forearms, legs, stomach, and cheeks. Strips of skin hung from the deeper scratches. Her fingers and nails were scarlet and bloody. She looked up at Cal and opened her mouth in a silent howl.

He could only stare at first, but then words came in a rush.

"Missy, Missy, what have you done? Honey, what have you done?" he asked, frantic. He jumped into the tub behind her and threw his arms around her, grabbing her wrists, afraid she would begin clawing at herself again. She didn't resist. But her sobbing grew louder, and tears ran down her cheeks, blending with the gouges until pink droplets began to fall from her chin, mixing with the dark reds that spotted the white tub.

Cal hugged her as Missy wept, his head against the back of her neck. Finally, she regained control of her sobbing and took a deep breath.

"You were right, Cal. I didn't understand it. But now, whatever it is, it's inside me. It's trying to control me. Giving me terrible thoughts. Terrible dreams. I want to get it out."

"Okay, honey. I'll help, let me get help, okay?"

"I couldn't get it out, but you can, right? You dig it out and then take it back. It needs to go back, Cal. It needs to fucking go back to where it came from. Make it go back!" she screamed hysterically.

Cal hugged her tighter and soothed her as best he could. As she sobbed in his arms, he wanted to tell her that it would be all right. He wanted to tell her that he'd get this thing—Kurriwilban or Koyorowen or whatever monstrous spirit it was—out of her and send it back home. But he didn't. Because he couldn't. Because the only way back he knew, he'd burned, at what he'd thought had been Missy's bequest. But, looking back, he was unsure if those words had been hers, or instead if they'd come from something desperate to stay here in this time, in this world.

Eventually, Missy's tears dried up and she grew alarmingly still. When Cal was confident she was back in control, at least temporarily, he eased himself out of the tub and found his phone. He called an ambulance, knowing that she would be taken from him when they came. But it was all he could do to help her. He was thankful, in part, for the shock that dulled his senses, because without it, he would certainly break down sobbing.

After the paramedics arrived and cleaned her up, they strapped her onto a stretcher and wheeled her out of the motel room.

Cal walked with her—fighting back tears, trying to be strong for her. He held her hand and looked down at her, hoping the expression on his face was reassuring. As they waited for the elevator, she smiled up at him, and he'd forced himself to smile back—but whether he was smiling at Missy or not, he could no longer say.

Storitel

Featured in Issue #75

...Ruth Gilbert

"Look, I can talk about it for hours, but the only way you're really going to understand is if you give it a go."

The Storitel lies on the bed, a spaghetti of wires and sensor pads. Nevin has the control panel, what he calls "the deck," and he's tapping something into the keyboard. He glances up at Ben.

"What do you say?"

Ben thinks of saying, _thanks but I'm not interested,_ just to see how Nevin will react. He's so sure of himself, this Nevin. His whole pitch has been conducted along the lines of "what a favour HealthMasters is doing you," and "how lucky you are."

"Okay," Ben says, really just to see if it lives up to the hype. And, after all, it's not like he's got a lot else to do.

Nevin attaches the sensor pads to Ben's head, two at the base of his skull, two at the crown and two at the temples.

"You'll need this," he says, handing Ben an eye shade like a cardsharp might wear.

Once that's on, Nevin stands back to view the effect. He grins. "Ready?"

Ben nods and Nevin presses a key on the deck. There's a click, a moment of darkness, a metallic buzz that resonates through his skull, and suddenly...

"You've got two days, and then I want you back here for the cargo load-up."

Mace Jadden looks over his scruffy crew, who aren't listening to a word he's saying, their eyes fixed on a horizon that's filled with liquor, the cards, and fancy pieces of purchased flesh.

"You go to a bawdy shop, then take your meds," he says, just to prolong the moment. "You get into a drunken fight and hauled off to chokey, don't give my name as sponsor. Cos there'll be no bailout. Hear me?"

With nods and, "aye Captains," they all peel away into the maelstrom of the Aktar Space Port. Two of them will end up in chokey, another will lose all his

"""

money at the tables, and three will come down with the Itch.

Mace grins and is just about to immerse himself in the seething mass of the breathing dock-side world, when he sees Totsy Rayd, with long hair now silver, but her face-glitter all smeared, yanking her arm from the grasp of a hulking long-haul tanker of man who is bellowing in her face.

Mace strides forwards, blood fizzing in his veins like a hit of jeven. It's been far too long since he last punched anyone, and since Totsy's aunt popped his cherry years back, this is a family obligation.

A blow to the stomach followed by a quick uppercut to the chin, and the thug folds to the ground with an *oof*. Totsy blows Mace a kiss before rushing off again to ply her trade, and Mace waves goodbye, heading for the Flying Festival Bar, where drinks are always half price to those who captain their own ships, and Netta owes him.

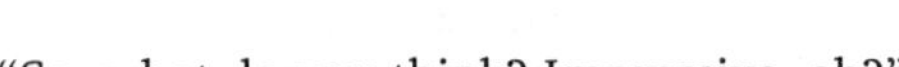

"So, what do you think? Impressive, eh?"

Ben lifts the visor; the mad rush of the space port now the stuffy warmth of the hospital ward, and for a moment Ben can't understand what he's doing there, lying on a bed, when he should be at the Flying Festival bar drinking jath and sweet-talking Netta.

"I know," Nevin says. "The brain can find it hard to handle the adjustment from one world to another."

He leans in close to remove the sensors, which come off with no sticky-tape rip, but just a gentle pressure as if they're attached by magnets, and Nevin's tangy aftershave replaces the muggy human scent of the space dock.

"What do you think?" Nevin asks again, folding the wires together with the deck and sitting back, looking at Ben with amusement.

Ben's trying to get over the smack-in-the-face reality to it. He's still flushed from flooring the thug and half-expects that if he looks in a mirror, he'll see a city mark tattooed down his face. Mace's face.

"First time for full immersion is always a bit of a shock," Nevin says. "More so if you're a rookie. What's new here is not the sensory surround. We've been doing that for years. The key here is the fact that you're inside the character's head and…"

Across the room Sandeep starts coughing. Ben takes a careful breath and hears the responding rattle in his own lungs. He looks down at his hands. His skin has shrunk to fit his bones, and his fingers are skeletal, the veins ridged and tight.

"…so it's a prototype. And we're hoping that this trial study will demonstrate just how valuable the game will be to people like yourself who are recuperating from a serious illness or a surgical procedure. We believe it may even speed recovery."

Sandeep's now surrounded by nurses. Rachel holds the IV flask, while Marcia grips a sputum bowl, scowling.

"Now we know that you're a HealthMasters client," Nevin is saying, looking down at a screen he's taken from his satchel. "And it's because HealthMasters and Storitel are owned by the same conglomerate that we're able to give you this opportunity."

"An opportunity" Nevin calls it now, when it's really their chance to try out their new game for free on a captive audience.

"I don't see…" Ben says, not wanting to offend.

Nevin looks up. "Yes?"

"Is there a story? Or is it just…" Just drinking and fighting in a sci-fi setting is what Ben wants to say.

Nevin looks perplexed. "Didn't I… Shit. I must have pulled you out before you got to the hook. Let's put you in again."

Ben is plugged back into the Storitel machine and…

Mace is taking a shortcut through loading bay 14 when he hears a yelp, a thunk, and then the sound of groaning, and he's running round the corner before his brain has caught up with his feet.

Between pallets of brick-protein two bodies lie in twisted positions on the ground. One is a thick-set burly man with a laser burn through his forehead. The other, a hard-faced blonde woman, has a wound to the left side of her chest, the red stain spreading in a widening circle as she presses her hand down hard, trying to stem the flow.

Mace whips off his jacket and crouches beside her, lifting her head, pressing his own jacket to the wound, though he can see from the loss of colour in her face and the way her eyes are turning glassy that she hasn't much time left. Still, she's whispering something, her final words, and he leans in close.

"Bomb," she says, but her voice is so hoarse he can't be sure.

"A bomb?"

"Here. Must find it." There's a bubble of blood at her mouth now. "Must defuse it. Not much time."

"Where?" he asks, but her head falls back like a broken puppet.

Mace looks round but…

"Ben." Nevin peers into his face. "How did that go?"

Ben's still wrenching his mind back into real life, away from the dying woman and the bomb that must be defused. "Good… fine."

"You'll be one of three people in this hospital who'll be trialling the game."

Nevin brings out a light-pen and screen from his satchel. "Just need your signature."

Ben can see Nevin's not expecting a refusal, but he's still unsure if he's up for this. It's not real life. It's a trick. Fake. And afterwards he'll still be here.

"Nurse!"

In the next bed Jamie's doubled over, gagging. No nurse gets there in time and a fountain of vomit smacks on the linoleum floor, acrid, nauseating. Nevin screws up his face in distaste, and Jamie heaves again and again.

"Okay," Ben says quickly.

Nevin produces the all-teeth, salesman smile and passes the screen and pen to Ben, who must sign in three places and give his permission for his photo and name to be used in publicity material.

"We've got one of the other players, Eric, in mind for the whole photo shoot thing," Nevin leans in close. "He's a Gold Class HealthMasters member." He takes the screen from Ben. "So we probably won't need you for that."

He tucks the screen into his satchel. As Marcia brings over a mop, muttering something ugly under her breath, Jamie glances over to Ben and gives a rueful grimace of apology. Ben gives him a no-big-deal shrug.

"Anyway, any problems, give me a call." Nevin whips a card from his pocket, hands it over and with a finger to his brow in a pseudo salute, he's out through the folding doors.

All the coughing Ben didn't do during Nevin's visit happens now. He folds himself over the side of the bed, gripping the bars, struggling to catch his breath. Out of the corner of his eye, he can see the HealthMasters envelope lying on the bedside table. It's been there all morning.

When the coughing's over, he picks it up. He stares at the fancy HealthMasters logo and the motto, *your health is our business*, for a long moment before sticking his finger under the flap and tearing it open.

Dear Mr Walker, in regards…

Ben scans the paper for the words and finds them halfway through the second paragraph, *treatment is still considered experimental… regret to inform you… not covered by your policy.*

He reads the whole letter, just in case he's got it wrong. But there's no mistake.

Fuck. He's finished now.

The afternoon wears on; thirty minutes of antibiotics through the IV, a flap of beef in gravy for dinner, and tinned fruit salad. More tests of his temperature and pulse. Evening bleeds into night. The ward is silent now, except for the usual heaving for breath, the padding back and forth of the nurse on night shift, and Jamie's snore. Ben coughs as quietly as he can. He glances at his watch. In two hours they'll be waking him up to take his temperature again. He looks over at the Storitel machine with its pads and wires.

Bloody HealthMasters. They won't give him the treatment, but they'll give him a game? Is it some kind of sick joke? Or is it just that Marketing and Treatment Approval don't communicate at all?

He's thinking of reading a book, anything to pass the time, when two men in black security uniforms complete with gun, cuffs, tear gas, and steel capped boots come marching into the ward. Right towards Ben.

He rears back against the pillows, which provokes a bout of coughing. By the time it's over, the men are at Jamie's bedside, shaking him awake.

"Health insurance's been pulled," one growls as Jamie blinks, still half-asleep. "Come with us."

And when Jamie makes no immediate effort to do so, they grab him by the arms, hoist him out of the bed, and frogmarch him towards the door in his pyjamas. Too startled probably to protest, Jamie is out of the door in seconds.

Ben's breath is coming in short gasps, half choking him. His whole body is shaking. He can't sleep now or read a book, but on the bedside table there's an out. Ben pulls the Storitel equipment onto the bed. He matches up the positions of the sensor patches with the diagram. He works out which keys to tap on the deck and…

Mace gazes down at the ground, but where there should have been two bodies, a pool of blood even, there's nothing there at all, yet he's only been away five minutes. He peers round to check if he's in the right place.

"You been drinking?" the burly Security man with the curly blond moustache demands. He grabs Mace by the chin and peers into his eyes.

"No, and I'm not spaced out or high." Mace yanks his face away from the man. "I'm on leave, with better things to do with my time than jerk you off. The woman said there was a bomb. She was lying here. She was bleeding out."

The second Security man, a skinny runt of a fellow, snorts then spits, leaving a gobbet of saliva glittering on the plasti-stuff deck. "Nutter," he mutters to his offsider. "Should chuck him into chokey."

"That'll just waste your time, waste mine," Mace says. "Buy yourself a drink officers, and we'll call it quits."

The runt scowls as if the twenty credits Mace is handing over is a fraction of what they are worth, but he takes it right enough. Blond Moustache scowls too and puts a hand to his gap-gun like he might blow Mace's head off given a second chance. Showy bugger.

They leave Mace staring down at the empty ground. He kicks at an empty packet of GinSing smokes. He knows what he saw, and he knows he's not stoked or shit-faced.

Is it mock-o-tainment? He glances round for cameras. That he sees none doesn't mean that they aren't there, but the punchline would have surely been delivered by now. Girls in sparkly dresses and a scoffing, chortling host. But nothing.

He leans against the stacks of brick-protein and frowns. How the hell is he going to find a bomb hidden somewhere in this massive space port? That's if it exists. If it doesn't, effort spent on the search is valuable drinking time gone to waste.

Mace has just decided to saunter on down to the Festival bar and maybe ask some questions while supping on a reviving bottle of jath, when a woman comes racing round the corner and runs smack into him.

"What the hell!" He jerks her away and sees she's a looker. Long black hair runs like liquid down her back. Purple eyes you could drown yourself in.

She steps forwards and jabs something hard and metal into his belly, and he looks down to see a gap-gun rammed up against his gut.

"See a girl here?" she asks. "See a tough-looking blonde girl?"

For a moment Mace just stares at her. Then he grabs her wrist, twists it up and round, pinching the nerve so she drops the gun and, yanking her arm up tight and hard, she lets out a stifled groan.

"Who are you?" he demands, "and what the hell's going on?"

"I'm Pilar," the girl says. "I'm looking for a bomb."

"Ben?"

The girl is staring at him, and he needs to know...

"Ben!"

The voice yanks him out of the game. He lifts the visor. Rachel, the nurse, the nice nurse, is waiting by his bedside. She's holding a tray of medication and gives it a meaningful look.

Ben unhooks himself from the game. He winds up the cords. He puts it on the side table. Jamie's bed has already been stripped and remade, neat as a pin, as if Jamie had never been there. Ben asks nothing. Rachel does the tests. He swallows the pills.

"You really should get some sleep," Rachel says. "I can give you tablets if you need them."

Ben agrees to a sleeping pill. Without it, the only option is the game, and HealthMasters has made enough decisions for him already.

His dreams are full of space travel, girls with silver hair, and gun fights, but he wakes to more medication, another round of obs, and breakfast. He's halfway through a bowl of lumpy grey mush posing as porridge, and a cup of lukewarm ersatz, when Jamie's replacement arrives. He has the smooth face of a man who's had work done, a shiny gold watch that he refuses to put into the beside cabinet, a loud voice that demands breakfast, a doctor, and a private room. And continues to demand them all morning.

The Storitel would be an escape but Ben grips his hands together and forces himself not to hook back in. He knows how addiction works and can read the signs. And because he's so desperate to return to the game, find out about the girl, the bomb, even have a few drinks at the Flying Festival bar, he resolutely leaves the Storitel equipment on the bedside table, even though it means he has to listen to his new neighbour's screen, which is playing an endless run-through of the news—famine, rioting, food shortages, and record levels of pollution—far too loud.

After a lunch of a flabby ham sandwich and a bowl of emerald green jelly, Ben manages a half-doze, but is woken by a feeling that someone is standing nearby. He jerks up in bed, panicked that it's a return of the security guards, but it's a round-faced Asian girl wearing pyjamas with cartoon sheep and towing an IV stand.

She glances over to the Storitel on the table. "You play game?" she asks, her voice quick and staccato.

He says nothing, but she leans over, extends her hand and says, "I'm Doris." Her nails are fluorescent pink, the polish scuffed. Her grip is surprisingly firm.

"Ben."

"You play Mace, right?"

He nods. He glances over to his neighbour, but he's finally asleep, and someone's turned off the screen.

She grins. "That fight so exciting. And now Keenan help us. He's nice guy. Good-looking. I think he's government man. But he find clue to bomb. So he's good guy."

She misreads the confusion in his face.

"I'm Pilar," she says. "Pilar in the game."

"Who's Keenan?" he asks warily.

Doris frowns. "You don't play? So avatar play you? Why? Game's fun. Better than here." She gestures to the ward, where Sandeep is hacking up something disgusting in a bowl, and Marcia is having a hissing argument with an orderly in the corner of the ward.

Ben picks on the easy question. "Avatar?" he asks.

Doris pulls over a plastic chair, sits down, and explains everything that Nevin hasn't. If you don't play when the others are playing, the game supplies an avatar stand-in. There are three player characters. Him, her, and a third, Keenan.

"I haven't met him," Doris says. "Not in real life." She squints at him. "When you stop play?"

"When Mace met Pilar."

"Okay, so then I tell you I look for bomb too. And then we find bodies…"

I don't care, he wants to say, but he finds her breathless enthusiasm engaging and doesn't want to deny her the obvious pleasure she takes in recounting to him the events he's missed, so he lets her run on.

"…and we get clue to bomb location from contact."

"Contact?"

"I have man who know things. He's my contact in brothel." She giggles, bringing her hand to her mouth. "Very funny, you in brothel when you…" She snorts with laughter. "…very funny."

Ben resists the temptation to ask what happened and why it was so funny.

He doesn't point out that she's talking about Pilar as if it's herself.

"Then we have big fight. And we meet Keenan. He help."

Ben nods. Off in the corner of the ward he can see Sandeep's wife is crying. A doctor hovers, looking awkward. It's bad news.

"Why you don't play?" Doris asks.

"It's too real," he says, surprising himself with the answer. "And better than here."

"Oh." Doris thinks about this. "Yes. Better. Fun." She rises to her feet. Her black fringe flips against her forehead.

"But what…" he can't stop himself from asking. "What was the clue?"

She grins. "Bomb maybe in Frying Fish bar."

"Flying Festival bar?"

"Yes."

It's so stupid. It's just a game. But he has a memory of Netta who owes him… something, he's not sure what, and he doesn't want the bar and Netta to get blown up.

The man in the bed next door is yawning and heaving himself upright.

"Nurse!" he bellows. "Goddamn it! Nurse!"

Ben picks up the Storitel deck. "Okay."

Doris grins again, and the smile lights up her face. He waits until she's out of the ward, then pulls down the visor, taps a couple keys, and…

Mace races down the alley after Pilar and Keenan. The heavy-booted men are close on his heels as he darts through the door of the Too Cute Hologram bar. Images of half-clad girls flicker and wink round him, and Mace leaps up onto a podium and runs through a flimsy curtain and up a narrow staircase, trailing yelps of indignation from girls in curtained cubicles lining the corridor. With Keenan and Pilar close behind, he climbs through a window, down to the street and into another bar where Terren, one of his crew, is busy losing half his stake money. From there, through the back door and out the gate and onto the dock, Pilar clutches the arm of a Security man and bats her eyelids saying, "Oh please, help me. My ex-husband has hired men. They have weapons. They're chasing me. Oh, do help me!"

And as the Security man's attention turns to their pursuers, he, Pilar, and Keenan race off round a corner, through a pawnshop, and end up in a grubby lane out the back of a bakery.

Mace catches his breath, inhaling the smell of just baked chuck-nut bread. He glances over at Keenan; big build, thatch of blond hair, good teeth, and with far too much of an eye for Pilar.

"Government man, you say?"

"Yes," Keenan agrees in clipped tones, straight off, like he's proud of it. "I'll take it from here. You can be about your business."

Now's the time to walk away. Keenan is paid for this. Mace is paid to get himself drunk and then sober before the next shipment is loaded. But the problem is, he wants to get drunk at the Flying Festival Bar. And that's where the bomb's supposed to be.

"I'm going with you," Pilar says, arms folded.

"Yeah," Mace agrees. "Me too."

Keenan opens his mouth to say something, then just nods. Mace senses a swift movement behind then hears a buzzing sound, and suddenly there's a fizzing on his neck, his whole body is one big vibration and then…

Ben pulls back the game visor. Around him the ward is business as usual. No one has called his name or demanded his attention, which would normally pull him out of the game. He checks the clock. He's only been playing for forty minutes; this isn't the three-hour maximum wake-up call.

He looks down at the machine. The controls all seem to be working, and all the sensor pads are still attached to his neck and forehead. But when he tries to put himself back in, a message flashes out: "YOUR CHARACTER IS TEMPORARILY OUT OF THE GAME."

What does that mean? This isn't a competition. How is he out?

He looks again around the ward. It's only mid-afternoon. Dinner isn't for another couple of hours. Obs has been and gone. His new, obnoxious neighbour is peering over at the Storitel equipment.

"What's this?" he demands, frowning.

"Nothing," Ben says, swinging his legs over the side of the bed. He'll find Doris. Maybe she can explain.

Rachel gives him directions to where Doris might be found. On the way he pauses for breath by a reinforced glass door that separates the private from the public ward. On the other side, as the security guard moves away, he sees a pool of blood on the grimy lino, and an arm dangling from a gurney. Then he hears the faint sound of screaming before the guard moves back into place, hiding everything from view.

By the time he reaches Doris's ward he's exhausted and still trembling, and half wonders why he's come, but there she is, in bed, reading from a screen, the Storitel equipment on the table beside her.

"Hey, Ben," Doris says, as Ben lowers himself into a chair. She tosses back the covers and swings her legs over the side of the bed. "You shut out of game too?"

Ben nods. "You know why?"

"That guy Keenan, he shot you," she says, kicking her short legs. "And he player character. He supposed to be with us on the team. So why he do that? It go totally against game rules."

Ben has never seen any game rules.

"Shall we go look for him?" he suggests. "He must be here in the hospital."

This gets a grin of approval from Doris. "Sure." She jumps to her feet, looking round carefully. "Quick," she says. "Before Nurse Allen see. She don't like people to leave ward."

The two of them sneak out, which is hard when Doris is pulling a squeaky IV stand and he's as breathless as a teenager on their first date. They have to check each ward, scanning beds and shelves for the Storitel equipment. It's in Oncology where they see a man, a skinny man, arguing with a nurse; the deck and the leads and the sensor pads an untidy pile on his blankets.

"Three hours is the maximum," they hear the stocky nurse say. "You have to take a break."

The man gives her the finger as she walks past Ben and Doris, and then frowns as the two of them approach.

"Hi," Doris says brightly, "We play the Storitel game with you. I'm Pilar but real name Doris. This Ben, he's Mace."

The man, who has a grey scratch beard and a gaunt, sallow face, gives a look of disbelief from one to the other, but he doesn't look like the burly, blond Keenan either.

Doris pulls out a chair and gestures to Ben to sit down, and he does because he's knackered, though Keenan is less than welcoming, muttering "Eric" just out of politeness.

"What you do in the game?" Doris asks. "You shot us. We can't play."

"Do you want to save the port on your own?" Ben asks. Stealing our thunder, he wants to say but doesn't. It sounds stupid. It's just a game.

"I'm going to blow up the space port," Eric says bluntly.

Both Doris and Ben stare at him.

"But that's not goal of game," Doris says. "And Keenan is government man, he should save space port."

The man hoists himself up against the pillows, scowling.

"To hell with the space port," he says. "Let it burn."

There's a moment of awful silence.

"Why?" Doris says simply, her eyes wide.

"I'm dying," he says. "Why shouldn't they?"

Doris says nothing at all. Neither does Ben.

"I've got a wife," Eric says. "I've got two kids. And I'm dying at forty-five. Forty-fucking-five! To hell with the game and to hell with HealthMasters offering me a toy like I'm a bloody kid. Like it's going to help."

Ben swallows hard. "Come on," he says to Doris and rises to his feet. "Let's go."

Doris chewing at her lip, nods. "I'm sorry," she says to Eric. "For everything. But good to meet you."

But Eric has already lost interest in the two of them, staring at the Storitel like he's ready to get back to it whenever the nurse's attention is diverted.

Back at Ben's ward, Doris suggests looking to see if his character is back online. It is.

"You want to play?" she asks him.

He does. He really wants to keep Mace alive. And when he nods, Doris gives that enormous smile again. No sound from Ben's neighbour, whose bed is now surrounded by curtains. Ben waits a lengthy ten minutes for Doris to get back to her ward and back in the game, then picks up the Storitel equipment. He pulls on the visor, taps the keys, and then…

"Hell, don't smack me," Pilar knocks Mace's hand away from her face and sits up. "What happened?"

"Keenan," Mace says. "Proves you can never trust a god-rotting government man." He pulls Pilar to her feet. "Come on, let's get to the Flying Festival Bar.'

They run hell for leather down grimy alleyways where girls on bawdy-shop balconies flap their flimsy peignoirs, and Totsy Rayn waves at him, grinning. Through the docks, past the assayers and customs, and finally they're at the iron-bound door of Flying Festival Bar.

Mace skids to a halt in the doorway. There should be a bustle of barmaids, the clink of glasses, the low and husky voice of Dekla at the microphone singing of her heartache. But there's an eerie silence interrupted only by the door banging shut behind them. A muscled man with an eye-to-jaw scar is standing there. Another big man is at the foot of the stairs that lead up to the rooms, normally rented by the hour.

"You Mace?" says the man at the stairs.

There's no sign of bloodshed, no upturned chairs, no smashed glass. Both the man at the door and the one at the stairs are holding laser rifles with an ominous familiarity.

"I've just come in for a drink," Mace says, strolling towards the bar as if nothing is wrong. "Where's Netta?"

The man at the stairs comes over slowly. Out of the corner of his eye Mace can see Pilar standing beside the big guy at the door. She gives a slight nod, and he twists over the counter, grabs a bottle of jath and smashes it down on Stair-Man's head. At the same time there's a howl of pain from the doorway, and Door-Guy is holding his crotch and gasping.

Mace grabs the rifle from Stair-Man. He races up the stairs and pauses on the landing, where Pilar almost slams into him. Which door?

Pilar points to one, cupping her ear, and Mace can hear it then, the noise of someone muttering something indistinguishable. On tiptoes they creep to the door and lean against it, listening. Someone—Keenan—is cursing. Fluently. Angrily. As time ticks away.

No time for finesse or stealth, they throw open the door and there's Keenan, crouching over a glass box filled with a tangle of filaments wound round a tube of bubbling blue liquid.

He grabs a gun just as Mace lifts his rifle, and it's a stand-off, Pilar frozen in the doorway.

"What the hell are you doing?" Mace demands. "You'll kill us all."

Keenan shakes his head. "There's still time." Slowly, he rises to his feet. "Move away from the door."

But Mace stands his ground. "Diffuse the bomb," he says. "There's no point to this."

"First step of revolution," Keenan says. "Disable all the ports. This is happening in every colony planet in the Federation."

The man's crazy.

"We're not going anywhere," Mace says. "It'll kill us all if you don't diffuse it now."

"Do you think I'm afraid to die for the cause?" Keenan demands.

"I know I am," Pilar says, and for a split second, Keenan's eyes flick to her. It's enough. Mace shoots, Keenan goes down, but there's a drilling pain through Mace's shoulder, and the sound of footsteps on the stairs.

"I'll deal with the bomb," Pilar shouts, "you sort out the company."

And though the pain is sharp as swords, he runs to the doorway and takes pot shots at Door-Guy and Stair-Man as they try for the landing.

Minutes later, Pilar yells, "bomb's out," and from below there's a shout of, "Security! Face down on the floor," followed by the sound of a shoot-out.

Pilar sits beside Mace as he collapses against the wall. She kisses him, cool and gentle on the lips.

"How did you know how to diffuse that bomb?" he asks as she draws back.

Pilar smiles at him. "Oh, I'm also with a rebel group," she says. "Just not one that wants to blow up the space port."

Mace opens his mouth to say more, and she places a finger on his lips to silence him.

"Let's get a drink," she says.

Best suggestion he's ever heard. She helps him to his feet and…

"Ben, it's time for your obs."

Ben pulls up the visor and lets out a deep breath. Rachel is standing by the bed. As he pulls the sensors from his neck and forehead and all through the tests, he's grinning.

"Everything okay, Ben?" Rachel asks, curious.

He nods. Fine. And it's true. He's breathing better, the ache in his chest seems to have vanished. He could go another round with Keenan if necessary, and maybe once he's out of this hospital, he'll join the police force, or the army, or become the captain of a ship transporting cargo long distance.

As Rachel pads off across the ward, Ben chuckles to himself. It's stupid. He knows that. But it's how he feels.

The man next door looks over and scowls. Ben grins at him. Then the swinging doors of the ward flip open, and Mike Nevin strides across the worn linoleum floor.

Nevin is beaming.

"Ben, you nailed it," he says, raising his hand to give Ben a high five.

The world of Mace and Pilar, Keenan and the Flying Festival Bar, is suddenly no more than the sediment of a dream, and Ben's bent over in a coughing fit that seems to last forever.

When he finally raises his head, Nevin looks up from his screen.

"Do you need something?" he asks, looking around as if he's vaguely aware that summoning help was something he should have done five minutes ago.

Ben shakes his head.

"So," Nevin says. "Pretty impressive stuff there in the game." He leans in as if imparting a secret. "You know, I got the impression at the beginning that you weren't too keen. But the time you put in, and the way the game evolved, I'm guessing that you got hooked. Am I right?"

Ben shrugs. "Sure," he says, as if it might happen to anyone, and he suspects it might.

"Okay, well things in the game didn't turn out exactly how we expected. In part that does show its versatility in being able to cope so well with the players' changing demands, but it also means that we can't use Eric Stanton for PR. He's one angry guy. And not that well, as it turns out."

Ben's surprised that they were ever thinking that Eric would promote the game, given his feelings about HealthMasters, or that Nevin's even complaining about Eric's illness, considering that they found him in the oncology ward, but Ben doesn't say so. He's waiting for Nevin's pitch.

Then it comes.

"So, we're giving you the opportunity to share your love of our game with the public." Nevin pulls from his satchel a cap with the words Storitel: the hero you always wanted to be, embroidered over the peak.

"The cameras should be coming in tomorrow morning. And the CEO would like to have a chat with you."

"No."

The word comes out short and sharp from Ben's mouth. It's so unexpected to Nevin that it shuts him up for five whole seconds.

"But we've given you…"

Ben is already reaching over to the bedside table. He thrusts the letter from HealthMasters into Nevin's face.

"Look," he says, in the peremptory tones more suited to Mace Jadden than himself.

It comes as something of a surprise to Ben that Nevin does as he's told. He reads the letter. Then he looks up.

"I don't quite…"

"HealthMasters shouldn't be wasting their money on games. They should be paying for treatment."

Slowly Nevin nods his head. "Well." He rises to his feet. "Maybe Ms Lee…"

"Doris won't do it either," Ben says firmly, though he can't be sure of that. "You'll have to trial the game again."

Nevin sucks at his lower lip. Maybe they have a schedule and a rerun doesn't fit into it. He looks down at Ben.

"And if I could get HealthMasters to review your case?"

Ben wants to shout, *yes, yes, then I'll do it!* But the devil-may-care bravado of Mace Jadden comes surging back to him.

"Yeah," he says, coolly. "Maybe then."

Nevin nods. He gives Ben a disapproving look, but Ben doesn't care now what Mike Nevin might think. And as Nevin disappears out of the swing doors, Ben's neighbour unexpectedly gives him the thumbs up.

"That's the way," the man says, and Ben nods and smiles as he gets out of bed.

He's going to find Doris and continue what Mace and Pilar started in the Flying Festival bar.

Contributors

TARA CAMPBELL (www.taracampbell.com) is a writer, teacher, Kimbilio Fellow, and fiction editor at *Barrelhouse*. She received her MFA from American University in 2019. Previous and upcoming publication credits include *SmokeLong Quarterly, Masters Review, Wigleaf, Jellyfish Review, Booth, Strange Horizons*, and *CRAFT Literary*. She's the author of a novel, *TreeVolution*, and two collections, *Circe's Bicycle* and *Midnight at the Organporium*. Her newest book, *Political AF: A Rage Collection*, was released by Unlikely Books in August 2020.

A lifelong science fiction and fantasy enthusiast, **RACHEL CHIMITS** works in Colorado as a writer and editor for World Challenge, Inc. Before that, she lived in Fuzhou, China and taught at a foreign language school. Her stories have also appeared in *Reality Break Press, Reunion: The Dallas Review, Speculative City*, and the anthology *If This Goes On*.

JENNIFER R DONOHUE grew up at the Jersey Shore and now lives in central New York with her husband and her Doberman. She is a Codexian and an Associate member of the SFWA, with work appearing in *Escape Pod, Truancy, The Future Fire*, and elsewhere. Her novella series, "Run With the Hunted," is available on Amazon and most digital platforms. She tweets @AuthorizedMusin.

EPHINY GALE is the author of more than two dozen published short stories and novelettes that have appeared in publications including *Beneath Ceaseless Skies, Constellary Tales*, and *Daily Science Fiction*. Her fiction has been awarded the Sundress Publications' Best of the Net award and the Syntax & Salt Editor's Award, and has been a finalist for multiple Aurealis Awards. More at ephinygale.com.

RUTH GILBERT lives and works in Adelaide, arriving there via a childhood and education in England and her twenties spent working in France, Holland, Italy, and Spain. She reads across the genres and writes mostly speculative fiction and fantasy, and, at the moment, she's between writing a murder mystery novel set in nineteenth century Adelaide and a fantasy novel set in the Quissian Empire. She cycles and swims, but she'll only watch sport if there's a decent backstory.

JIM GOURLEY is a writer in Tacoma, Washington, United States, safely distant from any murder hornets. He is currently working on his first young adult novel and several screenplays.

MICHAEL GARDNER is a public servant living in Canberra, Australia with his wife and two kids. He grew up in a small country town in Australia, which continues to find its way into his stories. His work has been published in *Writers* *of the Future*: Volume 36, in *Aurealis*, and in *Metaphorosis Magazine*. He has twice been a finalist for an Aurealis Award. You can find out more about him at www.michael-s-gardner.com.

FRANK HEBBEN is a multi-award nominated author in Germany. His latest work *Algorithm of the Sea*, a novella exploring the lives of a handful of post-apocalyptic survivors stranded in a hotel, came third for the Kurd Laßwitz prize, and has been nominated for the Skoutz Award.

EVAN KENNEDY is an Alabama native who reads so many fantasy novels that it took him twice as long as normal to earn his PhD in Psychology. His hobbies include video games, TV shows, an embarrassingly large boardgame collection, and full-contact sword fighting with foam swords. His short fiction has previously appeared in *Daily Science Fiction* and *Podcastle*. He lives in Alabama with his wife and his passive-aggressive rescue dog."

CAROLYN RAHAMAN writes and produces *The Twenty Percent True Podcast*, short stories about modern monsters, which is going into its 7th season. On her blog (twentypercenttrue.blogspot.com), she talks about folklore, what she's reading, and the writing process. She lives in Chicago with her husband and son.

A T SAYRE has been writing in some form or other for over three quarters of his life, ever since he was ten years old. From plays to poems, teleplays to comic books, he has tried his hand at pretty much every medium imaginable. For the last couple of decades his focus has been in filmmaking/scriptwriting, but recently he has returned to his first love, short stories. His work has appeared most recently in *Theaker's Quarterly*, *Analog Science Fiction & Fact*, *StarShipSofa*, and *Haunted MTL*. A more detailed list of his publications can be found at www.atsayre.com/fiction. Born in Kansas City, Raised in New Hampshire, he lives in Brooklyn and likes to read in coffeehouses.

ROSE WEST has had a lot of writing-related jobs (proofreader, copy editor, copywriter, and more), but loves writing fiction the most. Her short fiction has appeared in *Andromeda Spaceways*, *Mothership Zeta*, and *Wergle Flomp*; she currently lives in upstate New York. Website: Rosewestwrites.wordpress.com.

Aknowledgements

We would like to express our sincerest thanks to the following contributors:

Proofreaders:

Michelle Birkette, Laura Cesile, Mat Danaher, Tom Dullemond, Wayne Harris, Nick Marone, Brooke Munday, Jessica Nelson, Jessica Nelson-Tyers, Samantha Ryder, Joel Schanke

Editorial Team:

Jim Anderson, Michelle Birkette, Stephen Brewer, Sue Bursztynski, Ellen Coates, Tim Conder, Timothy Conder, Chelsea Croawell, Mat Danaher, Tom Dullemond, Heather Ewings, Anthony Ferguson, Madelaine Geary, Brad Gordon, Amy Gordon, Wayne Harris, Michelle Jelley , Dev Jeyathurai, Devin Jeyathurai, Craig MacKie, Adelle Mandile, Nick Marone, Brooke Munday, Jessica Nelson-Tyers, Mary Pearl, Joel Schanke, Cat Sheely, Emma Stewart, Kieran Tyers, David Versace, Calie Voorhis

Andromeda Spaceways Publishing Incorporated is:

Laura Cesile, Tom Dullemond, Anthony Ferguson, Amy Gordon, Wayne Harris, Nick Marone, Brooke Munday, Jessica Nelson-Tyers, Samantha Ryder, Joel Schanke, Tanya Smytheman, Mallory Thomas

Artwork

"The Etiquette of Mythique Fine Dining" and "The Pearls That Were His Eyes," by **ARTY PAGPIE**; https://www.patreon.com/artypagpie

Cover Art by **BROOKE MUNDAY**

*All other artwork from Pixabay. No attribution required.